The Ghost Horse of Galinas Moor

Amanda Aubrey-Burden

Published by New Generation Publishing in 2017

Copyright © Amanda Aubrey-Burden 2017

First Edition

The author asserts the moral right under the Copyright, Designs and Patents Act 1988 to be identified as the author of this work.

All Rights reserved. No part of this publication may be reproduced, stored in a retrieval system or transmitted, in any form or by any means without the prior consent of the author, nor be otherwise circulated in any form of binding or cover other than that which it is published and without a similar condition being imposed on the subsequent purchaser.

www.newgeneration-publishing.com

 New Generation Publishing

Prologue

The old man sat quietly in the darkness waiting; waiting and watching with a practice born of patience, for he'd done this many times before. And he knew with unshakable certainty that on this very night he would see the apparition that so haunted his heart; knew also that by doing so would bring him only sorrow.

He looked over at the sleeping form of his grandson Owen. Good lad, he mused, but not up to the sight of Galinas Moor's ghost – indeed there were few that were. . .

Many in the village dismissed the legend as a fanciful tale, a lame endeavour to curb their children from wandering too far, or as some would say, a bid to discourage passing gypsy folk. But the old man knew differently, and it was this knowledge that had sustained him through many a lonely vigil as he wondered if he was the only soul left who now bore witness and believed.

Turning back to the window he gazed out into a clear and starry night. His eyes travelled the miles of slumbering moorland and he remembered the day his father first told him the tragic tale, in particular his words of warning at the end.

". . . and you must never tell anyone outside of the *teulu*, do you understand me? It frightens people and there are some who would rather forget; we keep it to ourselves, see. It's a like a legacy, a secret, and I trust you to keep it that way. . ."

The old man smiled sadly and shook his head in the darkness. Aye and I've kept it that way, he thought, although Lord knows it's been more of a curse than a . . . and then suddenly he heard it!

O Arglwydd!

That eerily wretched and unearthly cry; knew it as he knew the sounds of the wind, had heard it in his darkest dreams and helplessly he shivered and trembled before it. The cry came again then again and with it the drumming of thunderous hooves. Clutching his blanket more tightly around him the old man leaned forward as the sounds grew nearer, knew what he would see, had seen it a thousand times or more, but he could no sooner have turned his face away if his life depended on it.

And then there it was...

Oh, poor demented creature!

He watched entranced as a magnificent stallion of the palest hue galloped wildly into sight.

As always he was struck by the sheer beauty and unparalleled presence of this ghostly beast that Time, for all its sovereignty could not diminish! For it was a creature of almost mythological proportions and never, in all his years had the old man beheld such splendour and assuredly he'd known many.

The horse galloped into ever-decreasing circles as it began to lose pace; ghostly flanks heaving, nostrils blowing and seemingly spent. But the old man knew the haunting well enough to know that it wasn't over yet, and as the phantom beast raised its head to emit another cry he could see the chains that bound its throat and as ever, he cursed the cruelty of man!

The creature now launched its whole being into a bout of frenetic fury as it bucked and plunged, wheeled and turned, all the while tossing its great head in a frenzied bid to cast off the chains that so possessed its soul. And as the beast screamed out its torment to a bleak and empty world, the old man wept unashamedly for his anguish and frustration were great.

How useless he felt! How futile it all was! Would there never be an end to this poor creature's suffering? But it was always thus. And there was nothing he could do than watch and weep, forever hoping that on nights such as these that he would sit until dawn and have witnessed nothing more than a starry night and a gibbous moon.

Through his tears the old man saw the first flickering of lights that danced in a multitude of colours around the ghost-horse and recognised them as the sign that the haunting would soon be over. And as though seeming to sense this, the beast rose upon its powerful hind legs and lunged out defiantly, great hooves pawing the air, eyes afire with unbridled fury as though declaring to the world; *See me for what I am for I will always fight! I will never give in!* And as though in recognition of this indomitable show of strength the old man half-raised a hand in salute. Slowly the kaleidoscope of lights grew nebulous and less defined as they swirled and spun shrouding almost lovingly the figure in their midst. The phantom beast was little more than the palest shadow as then, with a feeling of profound gentleness, the whole scene slipped noiselessly into the night...

The old man turned away from the window and sighed deeply. He did not know how much longer he could endure the sadness of this spectacle, for it sapped his strength and lowered his spirit, and yet he knew he would be compelled to do so as long as there was breath left in his body. Rising stiffly he made his way over to the bed and lowering himself down carefully drew the blankets over him as Owen breathed quietly beside him. Gazing at his grandson's form in the darkness the old man knew the time would soon come when innocence of what lay beyond these earthly planes would be destroyed forever once he was old enough to know the truth, but until then, he mused, let sleeping children lie as ancient ghosts awaken...

And then *she* came.

Chapter 1

Beth felt the first stirrings of apprehension as the train slowed and chugged into the tiny station that was little more than a halt. For waiting there was a lone figure that was leaning with ease against a small grey pony harnessed to a trap and she knew that they were waiting for her. They both cut a lonely almost poignant sight as they appeared gradually through the mist and the young woman smoothed her hair beneath the bonnet and straightened her skirts keen to make a favourable first impression. As the train finally huffed and puffed to a standstill, the old man left the pony's side and came forward with a kindly smile and Beth felt all of her nervousness dissipate as he opened the door and offered her his hand. She took it gratefully and stepped down on to the platform as the guard carried her large trunk across to the trap before depositing it in the back with a heavy thump.

"I'm Tegid, head-stableman at Galinas House, and you must be Miss Watson."

His voice was soft with the Welsh lilt, his manner courteous without being stuffy. Twinkling blue eyes gazed out of a lined and deeply-tanned face that had seen many summers. A great drooping moustache added a melancholy air but the smile that peeped beneath it was genuinely warm and Beth beamed back in return.

"Why, yes, thank you, I am."

As the guard made his way back to the train he clapped the old man on the shoulder and said something in Welsh before blowing his whistle as the train began to crank up.

Tegid made some jovial reply before taking Beth's travel bag and led the way to where the pony waited patiently. The mist had thickened slightly lending a gloomy almost oppressive air to the day, and after helping the young woman to her seat, the old man took his and offered her a rug which helped keep out the worst of the chill and then they wheeled about as the pony took up the pace.

Once they'd left the station the road forked and the old man took the left holding the reins loosely as the road became more of a path that wound its way up towards bleak and barren moorland. Beth looked around her but could see little in the grey murkiness yet she felt something akin to a strange uneasiness as the landscape unfolded before them and she suppressed a small shiver.

"Is the house beyond the moors, then?" she asked hopefully.

The old man shifted position and gave her a bemused glance.

"No, miss, the house sits on the moors and has done these past five hundred years or more. Just a mile or so further on and we'll soon be there."

"Oh."

The young woman didn't know what else to say. Little had been given about Galinas House when she had applied for the post. Just that it was not far from the border in quite an isolated location. But then her interest had been primarily for the role that had been offered and her pleasure in accepting a new opportunity that would take her away from the tedium of small-town life. Her only regret was leaving her mother, of course, *but a life in service would be better than in the mills, and you are bright and have had an education,* her mother had told her, *and who knows what could follow once you get your foot in through the door!*

Inwardly Beth smiled at the memory of her mother's bright-eyed optimism and desire to see her daughter spread her wings, and her reverie was interrupted by a rasping cry that came out of the mist as a small black shape ran out in front of them.

Unperturbed the little pony did no more than prick its ears and kept up the pace as the black grouse scuttled off into some undergrowth grumbling its displeasure.

"She's very good, isn't she?" Beth observed and her praise was rewarded by a slow smile.

"Steady as a rock, my Megan," the old man said fondly, "All of the Squire's children learnt to ride on her. You don't get much better than a Welsh Mountain pony, if it's a loyal nature you're after. Do you ride, Miss?"

"No, I'm afraid not. There wasn't much opportunity but I've always wanted to learn. Horses are such beautiful creatures."

"Aye, they are that," agreed Tegid and pulled an old pipe out of his pocket and popped it in the corner of his mouth. "And we have a stable full of them. I'm not making any promises, mind, but I will have a word with the Master, see if you can't have a few lessons whilst you're here. The house can be lonely living this far out on the moor. . ."

It was Beth's turn to look bemused. "Why you almost make it sound as though my tenancy of the position will be a short one!" she said lightly and watched as he expertly rolled the pipe through his moustaches from one end of his mouth to the other before replying.

"Well that would be because nobody has ever stayed in the post beyond a month or more Miss. . ." He gave her a quick glance, his face was unreadable.

"You mean there have been others in the post before me?" Beth said at last, and feeling emboldened added, "How many were there. . . if you don't mind my asking?" Her heart was beginning a slow-moving descent towards her stomach, her earlier sense of anticipation now clouded by doubt.

"Three or four, if you don't mind my telling,"

Suddenly the old man pulled on the reins and as Meg came obediently to a stop he turned and taking the pipe from his mouth said,

"Ah *Arglwydd*, but you seem like a nice girl, and maybe I should say nothing, but you strike me as *gwahanol,* and well. . ."

Beth looked at him questioningly. *Different! Her?* What on earth was he implying?

She waited for him to speak as the mist swirled and breathed around them like a living thing. Somewhere in the distance a golden plover called out mournfully and Beth suppressed a shiver.

"We have an old saying in Wales," he said quietly and the blue eyes that had danced and twinkled on her arrival now held a grave light, "'Better the rod that bends than one that breaks' He gave a curt nod and went on, "You will need to be able to bend like the willow in a Welsh storm if you wish to stay in that house, for there are many things within it that will prove testing for someone so young and inexperienced of the world. . ."

Beth met his regard steadily as she absorbed the hidden meaning behind these words. Intrigued rather than alarmed she sensed the warning within them and in a wary voice asked, "Why are you telling me this?"

The old man replaced the pipe between his lips and gave a brisk click to the pony.

"Because I like you," he said simply, "because there's something about you that I didn't see in the others and because I have a feeling you'll make a difference."

As the trap rolled forward Beth kept her eyes on the old man and he lost the sombre look as the twinkle returned to his eyes.

"We also have another old saying in Wales; Humour the wise and happiness will follow."

"Really?" Beth asked politely.

"We can but hope. Just lean with the wind and if it gets too strong, be sure to seek me out. You will always find me where the horses are when it gets too much in the house. Ah look, there are the lights! We are not so far now, Miss. *Dewch ymlaen*, come on, Meg!"

They lurched forward as Megan smartly picked up the pace and the change of subject left the young woman in no doubt that their odd little conversation was over. She turned her attention to the array of lights up ahead deciding to store his words of warning away to be mulled over later. That he had shown himself to be a kind man had been a pleasant surprise, yet having declared himself an ally before she'd stepped foot into Galinas House was as bewildering as it was comforting; but she was her mother's daughter in all doughtiness of the Welsh spirit and his words served only to gird her not to faze. And as she drew the travel rug tightly against the rushing mist, she kept her eyes on the lights as they grew nearer like disembodied lanterns held aloft by faerie hands.

The house loomed ever closer as the rough ground gave way to more cultivated parkland where in the gloom could be espied shrubs and bushes and over the way what looked like a large orchard and walled gardens. But it was Galinas House itself that commanded attention. Large, rambling and starkly grey it had evidently not been built to please aesthetically, for it had an ugliness about it that even the softness of candle-light beyond it's small mullioned windows failed to enhance.

As they drew up in front of the solid oak doors, one of them opened and a darkly-dressed woman stepped out. She was thinly-set and of middle-age. Greying hair scraped back into a bun gave her a severe appearance but the eyes were large and intelligent as they openly appraised this young woman as a new member of her staff.

Tegid helped Beth to alight and as he unloaded her trunk two maids appeared like magic and taking an end each disappeared back into the house all the while trying to sneak a look at the new arrival.

As Beth went to bob a curtsey, the older woman shook her head and said, "There's no need for that. Welcome to Galinas House, Miss Watson. I'm Mrs. Davis, the housekeeper. Please follow me and I'll take you to your room. Oh and Tegid?"

The old man heaved himself back into the trap and looked back enquiringly.

"There's some *cawl* left on the hob. Tell Mrs. Giles I said you could have it."

He nodded and shook the reins before casting a final glance at Beth whose eyes thanked him before Mrs. Davis ushered her into the gloom of the great hall.

"Your journey was not too taxing, I hope?" the housekeeper said as she led the way across the stone-flagged floor.

"It was not as bad as I thought and quite an interesting excursion, thank you, Mrs. Davis." Beth replied politely. Her eyes were wide taking in her new surroundings as they made their way towards a wooden staircase at the far end of the hall. Tapestries and all manner of shields and weaponry adorned the walls of the great hall, and taking precedence along the middle was the biggest table Beth had ever seen. It was flanked by long rough benches that looked equally as old, and the burnished wood gleamed and glimmered in the firelight cast from the mighty hearth. As they passed by the great fiery maw Mrs Davis gestured towards it saying,

"We keep the fire going all year round in the great hall. It is a very cold house as you will discover, for moorland weather can be less than kind; even during the summer months."

No sooner had she spoken than a door behind the staircase opened and a young boy emerged carrying a basket full of logs. The Housekeeper paused and watched him with a keen eye as he scuttled over to the fireplace before emptying his load into the large metal box. He pulled his forelock respectfully at Mrs Davis and cast a shy look at Beth before scurrying back the way he'd come.

"That's Owen, Tegid's grandson. We have about twenty servants in the house all told; not that you'll come into contact with all of them, I'm sure."

The Housekeeper had begun to climb the stairs, one thin hand clasping the smooth worn wood of the handrail. "There is a staircase at the rear of the house for the servants who live in, but as you will be accommodated in the nursery wing you will not be expected to use it."

Beth was grateful for the information. Her mother, who had once been a lady's maid, had drummed into her the importance of knowing your place in such establishments, and as her position was particularly unusual, any enlightenment she could glean at this stage of her arrival would be of immense value.

As they reached the top Beth now found herself on a deep crimson carpet that led off in both directions to the two wings. Mrs Davis paused and nodding to the right said,

"That is the East wing of the house where the family live and have their bedrooms. The nursery and your quarters are in the West wing. Nanny Gwyn also has her rooms there as does the Governess and your charge," At Beth's look of confusion she frowned and said, "Yes, what is it?"

The young woman hesitated for a moment unsure whether give voice to the question that rose to her lips, but then the situation was unusual and she had to know at the risk of appearing impertinent.

The children, I mean, the other children of the house; do they not reside in the nursery, Mrs Davis? Forgive me if I am intruding but. . ." she trailed off as the housekeeper pursed her lips and a shuttered look came into her eyes.

"The family's children have their rooms in the East wing, Miss Watson that is all you need to know. Now if you would care to follow me I will show you to your room."

She turned on her heel and led the way down the dim hallway made even darker with thick wood panelling and Beth followed on knowing she had caused offence. But it was standard for children of great houses to live in the nursery quarters until they came of age, and so why they should be housed apart from their young relative Beth could only wonder. But further questions would have to wait for the housekeeper was speaking again as she pointed out the door to Nanny Gwyn's quarters, and then across the hallway to those of Miss Meacham, the children's governess.

The hallway curved round at the end towards another flight of stairs that took them up and round to a wide landing with several doors leading off. Reaching out to the first one Mrs Davis turned the heavy knob and walked briskly into what could only be described as a plain but comfortably-sized room.

A fire burned merrily in the grate and with a good stock of logs next to it. The furnishings were old, heavy but functional, and the bed had a tester from which hung heavy green drapes, matched by the curtains in the window. A ewer of hot water and a bowl sat on a small washstand with some linen beside it, and next to an ottoman unopened was Beth's trunk.

"Do you need any help with your unpacking, Miss?"

"No. Thank you. I'll be fine, and the room is lovely," Beth smiled uncertainly keen to regain lost favour with this stiff-backed ruler of the house. "Thank you kindly, Mrs Davies."

The housekeeper nodded and giving the room a final sweep before saying,

"The Master will see you at five o'clock sharp in the library. One of the maids will collect you and show you where it is. In the meantime I'll have some light refreshments sent up. Dinner is at eight. I will also arrange for a tray to be sent to your room. Just for tonight. No doubt Nanny Gwyn will have her own ideas of dining forthwith. . ."

Again there was that pursing of the lips and air of barely-suppressed disapproval. Beth could see that she would have to tread lightly with Mrs. Davis as Tegwen's words came back and resonated within her. Petty differences and power struggles were all part of the course in service but Beth hadn't expected to be privy to such quite so soon.

As soon as the housekeeper left the room Beth threw off her cloak and bonnet and went to the window interested to see what lay beyond.

The mist was lifting, and although the last vestiges of the day retained the dull greyness, there was still enough light to see the moors stretched out before her, as far as the eye could see. The embrasure had a window seat and Beth lowered herself down on to the cushion as she surveyed the dour and lonely landscape intently.

Having been raised in the latter part of her life in the small but bustling town of Brecon surrounded by lush green countryside, Beth had never known such a stark comparison, and although she didn't know why, something about the moors that repelled as much as they drew her. But she was a practical girl despite the inherent Welsh love for myth and mystery, and knew that it was the contrast she found fascinating and wondered how far the nearest village was.

She held that thought as a knock at the door heralded her tea-tray ferried in by a rosy-cheeked maid with a shock of red hair that was barely restrained by her cap. She had a friendly smile and a mischievous look and Beth warmed to her immediately.

"Tea for you, Miss, and some of Cook's griddle cakes baked especially!"

Beth rose from the window seat and came across for a closer look.

"Why they look delicious!" exclaimed Beth enthusiastically, "Can't think of anything I'd like more."

The maid beamed.

"Put it down here on your table, shall I, Miss? I'm Gwen, by the way!"

"Thank you, Gwen."

They regarded each other for some moments. They were much of an age, although their stations of life, despite being in service, were as like the sun and the moon, but there was an instant recognition between them of a kindred soul, and as though in acknowledgement of this, the young maid gave a small nod before saying kindly,

"Must all be a bit strange for you, Miss. I'll make sure it's me that comes to take you to the Master. And don't you worry now because he's a nice master; a very kind man you'll see!"

She beamed again and then with a quick bob took herself out the door before Beth could respond.

She shook her head in bemusement. Already the quirks of the people she would be working alongside were strongly in evidence and she hadn't been here a day!

As she sluiced her face and washed her hands she wondered what her mother would make of it. And as she sat down to partake of some tea and the cakes that were still warm, her thoughts then turned to her father and she had no doubt of exactly what he would have thought about it.

Although she'd loved her father dearly, he was a strict God-fearing man who had come from a well-to-do but impoverished family in Oxford. Forced to make his own way in the world he had become a curate and had met her mother in the course of parish duties near the estate where she worked.

Love can be a strange thing, and indeed it was an odd magic that drew the serious-minded young man into matrimony with the vivacious woman that was her mother. Beth considered the dynamics of their union often, and the story of how her father was offered a position near the growing town of Newport, and their joy when she had come along not long after. Their life of simple but contented bliss until the cholera epidemic of 1847 swept through the county and the tragedy when in the midst of his duties her father was struck down and returned to God.

Beth was fourteen at that time and her mother, with her indomitable spirit, wasted no time in removing them both from the growing crisis and they went to Brecon where her grandparents had a small-holding.

They were welcomed with open arms by her *Nain* and *Taid* who made room for them in their comfortable cottage, and a tiny pension that her mother received on her father's demise was subsidised by taking in occasional needlework and they had managed Life was different, but unlike the thousands who had been bereaved and left transient by the epidemic they weren't destitute but it had been a difficult few years and life seemed all the more precious for having escaped the clutches of the dreadful disease.

Her mother had ensured Beth received as much education as she could administer, determined that her daughter would have the best chance possible making something of herself. It was an endearing but fanciful dream, for there was only ever one course open to a young woman of no means; a lifetime in service, or a different kind of drudgery in the great noisy mills that were springing up around the country. Beth knew which path she would prefer, so when her mother had learned of this position she drafted the letter of application herself telling Beth that such an opportunity was not to be missed.

"Better to be a companion than a governess, cariad," she'd enthused, *"and your charge is quite young; unusual, but it could be to your advantage and you'll have greater freedoms I'd imagine. And who knows? Make a favourable impression and show how versatile you are and you may yet step up the ladder to become Lady's maid!"*

Beth shook her head fondly at the memory and then roused herself to change out of her dress and tidy her hair. Unlocking the trunk she drew out a plain but serviceable dark grey dress with cream lace at the collar, one of the two new dresses her mother had scrimped to provide from her meagre savings.

There was a tall burnished mirror in the room that Beth now stood before as she unpinned her fair hair that tumbled thickly to her waist. With an expert hand she smoothed and coiled the rippling mass until it was returned to its former state and she regarded herself for some moments in the hope she'd pass muster.

She was very much like her mother being of medium height and possessed of a slim neat figure. She'd also inherited the masses of honey-blonde hair, but her eyes were her father's; deep-set, dark and expressive. As beautiful as *Nest* of legend, her Taid would say proudly, and Beth would laugh and shake her head at the comparison. Fortunately she'd also inherited her father's no-nonsense view of life and so laid no claim to false vanity.

She was nineteen years old and this was her first foray out into the world. She had hopes of making a success of what was her first stint of employment – no matter what the old man had said, for Beth was nothing if not a determined young woman, and spirited enough to ensure that whatever winds may blow in this house and from the people within in; she would be willing to bend certainly, but never enough that she would break. She knew little about her charge other than she was an orphaned relative and that there were 'circumstances' around her 'disposition', the full details of which would to be made clear upon taking up the position.

That Beth would only be in full possession of the facts until after her appointment spoke of a situation that was evidently sensitive and this only served to heighten her mother's speculation that there was a scandal involved in some way and impressed on Beth the need to be equally mindful.

"You know not what you are going in to exactly, Beth, but I think we can safely assume that the situation will require the utmost discretion. For I have never seen an advertisement worded so vaguely, nor a post whereby the conditions and the duties will be communicated after *the appointment. Most unconventional! But I'm sure they must have their reasons. . ."* And there had been a worried look in her eyes.

Beth preferred to withhold judgement until she had full possession of the facts. Another characteristic of her father's, but she was no less intrigued and was looking forward to meeting her charge and learning, finally, what lay behind the mystery.

There was a tap at the door and Gwen popped her head round.

"Are you ready, Miss? They're waiting for you."

Beth lifted her chin and turned to face the maid and smiled. There was a fluttery feeling in her stomach but she steadied this sudden onset of nerves and moved forward confidently.

"Yes, Gwen," she said and took a deep breath, "I most certainly am!"

Chapter 2

The maid led the way swiftly holding a candle against the gloom. The last vestiges of daylight had finally succumbed to the claws of a late winter that was reluctant to release its hold, and as they came to the stairs that led down to the main hall great scones had been lit casting eerie shapes across the stone-flagged floor.

There was a strong scent of age and beeswax that Beth hadn't noticed before so taken up had she been by the visual; and the hall looked different somehow, as though illuminated by something more than the soft candlelight.

They descended and Gwen looked back at Beth before bringing her to one of the doors that led off from the hall and she gave it a quick knock before entering and saying,

"Miss Watson, Sir."

As Beth stepped past her the maid retreated closing the door behind her.

A man of middling height with thinning hair stood before the elaborate fireplace with his hands behind his back. He was smartly but sombrely dressed and there was an air of sadness about him as he regarded Beth almost mournfully. Near him sat perched in a fireside chair was a very old woman of a much brighter countenance and by her dress and manner Beth guessed that she must be Nanny Gwyn. The old lady smiled and nodded almost as though reading her thoughts the Squire gestured to the opposite chair and said,

"Miss Watson, please be seated. I hope that everything has been done to make you comfortable since your arrival?"

Beth moved across and lowered herself down slowly into the over-stuffed chair aware that she was under close scrutiny.

"Yes, thank you, Sir, very much so."

She sat demurely, her hands in her lap and waited.

"This is Nanny Gwyn whom you will be working with on occasion; Nanny has been in our family since I was a boy, and although the children are now of an age they insist such care of themselves is no longer warranted; I, however, am inclined to disagree, and so Nanny Gwyn is retained as a privileged servant and will always have a place with us for as long as she wishes."

He broke off and glanced at the old woman fondly and Beth knew instinctively that it was for himself that he'd made the arrangement. That there was obviously a strong bond that existed between them was made apparent by the warmth with which his look was returned, and having an opportunity to observe her new employer more candidly in that moment, Beth took in the weak chin and weariness about the shoulders that denoted a man weighed down by something but... *what?*

Nanny Gwyn was looking at her again with that knowing stare, the small eyes as kind as they were canny and Beth smiled back with a small nod. But she couldn't help wondering where the mistress of the house was and why she was not present; or perhaps Beth's position was so menial it did not merit the attendance of both.

The Squire was clearing his throat as though what he was about to say would give him discomfort and then paused for some seconds as the fire crackled behind him and a clock ticked steadily on the mantelpiece.

"Your charge; my niece, came to us under unfortunate circumstances," he began in a strained voice, "indeed tragic circumstances, if I am to be honest. But Nanny Gwyn will apprise you of those circumstances in due course because servants will tattle, and I would have you know the truth as it stands and on good and trusted authority."

Surprised by this opening speech Beth glanced across to the old woman but she was looking into the fire with an expression that was carefully set and unreadable.

"But before I go any further, first I must insist upon your word, and as an added measure of respect for the personal nature of this matter, your willingness to sign a legal affidavit."

He paused again and looked at Beth expectantly as though awaiting a response.

The young woman was suffused with confusion; she had not been expecting *this!* Once again her eyes went to the old woman but her gaze remained on the fire and Beth knew she was on her own.

" I am afraid I must insist. . . does this present a problem, Miss Watson?"

The Squire kept his gaze upon her, his expression a mixture of hopefulness and what looked like regret. The oddness of his demeanour only served to increase Beth's feelings of disquiet, and yet in amidst them she sensed that this was a heartfelt imposition, a sincere measure designed only to protect, and she found herself shaking her head.

"No, Sir, not at all." She said.

He breathed out as though he'd been expecting a refusal and then gesturing to the small table near to Nanny Gwyn, added,

"The document is here, if you would be so good as to read it through and affix your signature."

Beth rose and walked over to where a thick parchment sat with pen and ink. She picked it up, scanned it quickly, and was relieved to see that it was nothing more sinister than an assurance she would not divulge details nor breach confidentiality, and then taking up the finely honed quill she dipped it's nib into the ink and signed her name carefully.

Without further ado the Squire sanded the sheet and then rolled it up before depositing it into a leather case. Beth returned to her seat, and this time Nanny Gwyn met her eyes and there was a glimmer of gratitude in them that intrigued Beth even more.

The Squire had returned to his former position and again made a nervous clearing sound in his throat.

"The child is the daughter of my only sister; no longer with us, I'm afraid, may she rest in peace. . . the child is also illegitimate."

Beth had suspected as much, as had her mother, but was surprised nevertheless at the directness with which this confirmation was imparted.

"We. . . I took her in for there was nowhere else for her to go and I would not, for love of her mother," his lip trembled slightly, "see her child go into an orphanage, or even, God forbid, the workhouse so she resides here with us," his voice grew stronger as though he was anticipating some kind of resistant response, "and she will remain residing with us until suitable arrangements can be made for her future."

He gave a small nod as though to himself and went on.

"The circumstances under which her mother passed away were extremely traumatic, to say the least, and the effect this has had upon the well-being of my niece has been considerable; For not only has she lost the power of speech due to the shock, but she also remains in a state of profound depression. Thus far all endeavours to rouse her from this. . . *fugue*," he cast a sympathetic glance at Nanny Gwyn, "have been in vain, despite the best efforts of Nanny Gwyn, for the child is so deeply embedded in her misery as to be completely unreachable."

He sighed with feeling.

"Understandably we have serious concerns for her mental well-being; therefore, as Nanny cannot be expected to carry such a burden alone, a more proactive approach is required, which is where you come in."

He turned now and fixed Beth with an almost apologetic look and in that moment she realised that here before her was a man who was essentially kind and possessed of a soft heart. It was also apparent to her that the predicament he found himself in was of no small distress, and any worries she had of being under the employ of a cold and stiff-necked master melted away as she recognised him for the good soul he was and she felt an unexpected sense of relief.

Nanny Gwyn also had that same ambience around her and Beth could only wonder why the old man Tegid had seen fit to warn her when all she'd received since she arrived here was considered kindness. She was mystified and even more intent as to the situation she now found herself in.

"The child needs attendance in abundance; companionship, stimulation, to be drawn out of herself and brought back to some semblance of. . . of. . . "He threw up his hands and looked to Nanny Gwyn appealingly.

For the first time the old lady spoke. Her voice was a gentle cadence of a Welsh lilt, the tone quiet and measured. As she spoke Beth leaned forward so she could hear her more clearly.

"I am afraid that the child has sustained such a shock that all forms of engagement need to be gentle and undertaken with extreme patience. We have tried everything within our means but still she refuses to speak and barely eats enough to feed a mouse. It is as though she has removed herself away from the world completely, and we need to bring her back, Miss Watson, before it is too late."

"Has a doctor seen . . ?" began Beth disturbed despite herself. She had heard of people overcome with grief, indeed she and her mother had worn the mantle for some time after her father died; but to be so wretched that you couldn't shrug it off and simply gave up!

"Yes, of course," interjected the Squire, "but they are at a loss as to the best course of treatment. Doctor Morgan has recommended that we try to shock her out of her shock, so to speak! But Nanny Gwyn has forbidden anything so. . . drastic! And I have to say that I agree. Doctor Lewis, however, who is newly qualified and his junior partner recommend a more modern approach. He suggests we persist slowly and in a more genteel manner by reading to her, trying to elicit interest in her surroundings, talking to her and demonstrating empathy for her plight."

"Which is why we chose you, Miss Watson," Nanny Gwyn said simply. "We understood from your application that you yourself have had personal experience of bereavement, and as such will be able to offer a greater understanding, or so it is hoped. . ." she broke off and smiled tenderly, "My condolences for the loss of your father, by the way, Miss Watson, I believe he was taken by the cholera some years ago, yes?"

"Yes," Beth replied quietly and was touched. The Squire made another sound in his throat that may've been a grunt of sympathy before saying, 'Pray, continue, Nanny.'

"This child needs a level of love and attention that unfortunately I am too old and arthritic to provide, but I will be on hand to assist and will be able to take care of her on your free day. It is a demanding role, Miss Watson, I will not pretend otherwise, and there have been others who have found the role too much, and so we endeavour in the hope that the right person will come along and if I am not to be mistaken, Miss Watson, I believe that person may well be you."

As Beth's eyes widened in surprise Nanny Gwyn nodded knowingly and then looked up to the Squire and gave a small smile.

"What say you?"

"Nanny," he replied with some animation in the tone, "you are rarely, almost never wrong and so why would I doubt you now! Miss Watson, you will soon discover that Nanny Gwyn is a remarkable woman with an excellent eye for people, and if she says that you will be up to this task then I dare to hope that my niece will be comforted by your presence, and God willing, brought back to where she belongs!"

Feeling rather dazed and not a little perturbed by this sudden and supreme confidence in her abilities, Beth looked to one and then the other not really sure what to say. If she had ever been in doubt of the close bond between the Nanny and her employer, the readiness with which he deferred to her was in itself an incredible insight. Small wonder the housekeeper had cause for some resentment, Nanny Gwyn was obviously an extremely privileged servant and it would do well for Beth not to forget it.

Finally she found her tongue, stumbling just slightly.

" I am most grateful for your faith in me; indeed. . . I. . .I am quite at a loss what to say, other than I hope that my efforts will not disappoint you and that I can only promise to do my very best."

Nanny Gwyn stood up and came over to Beth. She was small and plump and moved painfully. Beth rose and took the proffered hands as the old lady beamed up into her eyes, her face a criss-cross of lines, but the cheeks were still smooth and had pinked with pleasure.

"I'm afraid you must forgive us our enthusiasm, Miss Watson. We are guilty of putting you under undue pressure, I know, but you indeed have a quality about you that tells me you are more than capable and not afraid to try. The past year has been. . ." she paused and the sweet face crumpled just slightly, "difficult. . . for all of us. But please, we ask only that you apply yourself to the task with good intent and compassion and the rest, as the master says, will be in the hands of God."

"I can only say that I will do my best," said Beth earnestly and the old lady smiled and nodded releasing her hands.

"Miss Watson, I appreciate this has been much to take in but rest assured Nanny Gwyn will ensure you have all of the advice and support you may need. It has been agreed that you shall meet with my niece tomorrow. My wife. . ." a pained look flittered across the Squire's features and a harsh edge came into his voice, "is often indisposed and keeps mainly to her rooms. You will, at some point, meet with her, of course, but your duties are strictly confined to the care of my niece and nothing else; do I make myself understood?"

His change of tone and subsequent assertiveness took Beth aback just slightly for this was the first indication that there was perhaps more to this situation and its impact upon the house. She glanced at Nanny Gwyn who had hooded her eyes and gave an imperceptible nod.

"Yes, Sir." She said obediently.

"I am frequently away on business," he continued, "but Nanny Gwyn will keep me informed of any developments, and it is to her and her only, that any issues you may have are to be reported. Have you any questions, Miss Watson?"

Beth shook her head mutely.

"Very well, then I will leave you to the tender mercies of Nanny Gwyn."

His voice had lost that edge and he held out his hand surprising Beth further. She took it tentatively and he gave a small ineffectual shake.

"Welcome to Galinas House, Miss Watson. Let us hope that you will last longer than the others and that your endeavours will be successful."

He turned back to the fire and held his hands out to the flames. She was dismissed. Nanny Gwyn took her elbow and walked her to the door.

"Will you be able to find your way back, do you think, or shall I ring for a maid?"

"I will be fine, thank you, er. . ." Beth looked at her momentarily nonplussed. What was she to call her?

"Nanny Gwyn," said the old lady kindly, "Or Nan. I am happy to be addressed by either." She placed her hand briefly on Beth's sleeve. "I will come and collect you shortly. I thought we could have dinner together in my room. It is your first night; it will give us the opportunity to get to know each other."

There were untold secrets in the faded blue eyes that Beth knew would be imparted as soon as they were alone. As the old lady opened the door for her she murmured her thanks and stepped out from the warmth of the library. Her mind was racing; full and flurried with so many questions one in particular that was the most significant of all.

Not once had the young girl been referred to by her name! She had been spoken of as 'the niece' 'the child' or 'your charge' – even by Nanny Gwyn! And Beth had been struck by that, for the old nurse seemed especially kind and genuine in her concern for the young girl's plight.

The Squire had also demonstrated obvious worry and with affection, and yet not once had either of them deigned to call the child by the name that was given. Mystified Beth decided that would be her first question to the old nanny at the earliest opportunity!

Finding herself alone in the great hall she took the time to look around her and breathe in the very age of the place for it was the oldest part of the manor house and atmospheric in its lineage. Great shields and massive pikes glinted in the firelight as leopards leaped and unicorns fled amidst the beautiful tapestries, and as the candles bobbed and weaved from the array of table pewter. Beth thought she saw movement near the great doors and turning her head to look more closely saw only pools of darkness and tutted to herself impatiently. But as she walked across the great hall towards the stairs a chill came over her and she hurried to her room glancing back only briefly as she sensed eyes on her retreating back as though unseen figures kept vigil in the shadows.

Back in her room she shook off what she saw as an impromptu flight of fancy. The house was old and doubtless steeped in history, particularly being so close to the Welsh Marches, and her encounters thus far with its occupants had been somewhat settling, to say least. No wonder she was jumping at shadows!

Keen to return to matters of a more mundane nature Beth was pleasantly surprised to see that the fire had been banked up and her belongings unpacked. Gwen, she thought and gave a small smile. Going across to the bedside table she took up her book where the maid had thoughtfully left it with the idea she would read for a while until dinner. Looking at the small watch pinned to her bodice she saw she had ample time to revisit the debatable delights of 'Vanity Fair' for at least half an hour.

The book had been a going away present from her mother that would never have been allowed had her father had still been alive. For although he had always encouraged Beth to read and broaden her mind, his taste in literature differed widely from her mother and so it was a certain amount of guilty pleasure when she dipped into its pages and apprised herself with the exploits of Becky and Amelia.

"It will keep you amused and perhaps give you a more rounded view of the world in which we all seek to flourish. Just don't allow the aspirations of its characters to influence you, although you are far too much of a wiseacre to permit that." Her mother had said with a twinkle in her eye.

Pulling a chair up to the fire, Beth could think of no better way in which to ground herself away from the strangeness of her surroundings than by immersing herself into one just a little more familiar, and as she delved into story she lost all sense of time until a soft tap at the door announced the arrival of Nanny Gwyn.

Beth stood up and replaced the book next to the bed as Nanny beckoned that she follow her, and as they descended the stairs Beth was aware that she was on the cusp of knowing family secrets and for no reason that she could fathom, there came over her a reluctance to know more, because then she would be truly drawn in. Why she should even entertain such a thought was disquieting to her, for it was her mother who professed a certain 'sensitivity' from her side of that family. Beth was more pragmatic believing only in what her eyes would see and had her father to thank for that.

It's this house, she thought, I have been here not a full day and yet it is a place full of shadows that could play games in the mind of anyone! And as she followed Nanny Gwyn into the privacy of her quarters, she deliberately pushed down a sudden sense that the house seemed to harbour an unspoken sorrow, for she was not like her mother in that way, *she was not!*

Chapter 3

Nanny Gwyn's special status was even more defined by the comfort and convenience of her chambers. The sitting room was snugly appointed and even had a little stove from which a kettle bubbled quietly. A small table was simply and nicely laid for dinner with two plates sat covered and waiting, and two comfortable armchairs flanked the hearth from which a generous fire crackled and danced adding to the general feel of congenial cosiness.

A large thick rug covered most of the floor and a door led off from behind a curtain beyond which Beth assumed must be her bedroom.

She looked around appreciatively at the small pictures adorning the walls and a small Welsh dresser filled with wot-nots and the old lady's trinkets and treasures. It was not a grand room by any means, but in comparison to the dreariness of the vast library, it emanated warmth and homeliness that was reminiscent of the home she had left and Beth felt the unmistakable pang of *hiraeth*.

"Sit yourself down, Miss Watson, you must be famished, I'm sure." said Nanny Gwyn, "the house may be cold and we may want for warmer weather at times, but we've an excellent cook who ensures we eat well and that there's plenty of it!

Removing the plate covers both women were presented with slices of roast beef and a medley of vegetables and Beth was pleased to see that Nanny was not exaggerating. The plate was heaped full, and after saying grace there was little conversation as justice was done to the food.

As they were finishing up a thought suddenly occurred to Beth, and of the belief that Nanny Gwyn would not be offended by her giving voice to it she asked, "Miss Meacham, the governess; will she be eating alone in her room?"

Nanny Gwyn gave a small shake of her head. "No. Miss Meacham is a distant but impoverished relative of the mistress. As a courtesy she is allowed to dine with the children."

"In the nursery?"

"In the main house." said Nanny and dabbed her lips with the napkin." Miss Watson," and she bestowed on Beth what could only be described as a sympathetic look. "This is an unusual household that does not, in some ways, follow conventional standards. There are reasons for this, of which I will enlighten you shortly, but first let us retire to the fire and make ourselves comfortable. Can I offer you some tea?"

"Yes, that would be wonderful, thank you."

As Beth moved to the hearth and sat down, Nanny Gwyn pulled on the bell-rope and then busied herself at the tiny stove. Soon a maid with a sallow face appeared and gathered the dinner dishes on to the large tray she'd brought with her. She kept her eyes down as she did so, her obvious shyness in stark contrast to the forwardness of Gwen.

"Thank you, Mary." said Nanny and placing a small table in front of the fire she soon had the tea poured and gestured for Beth to partake of milk and sugar.

Soon they were alone again and for some moments there was an easy silence as each one looked into the fire and marshalled their thoughts, then as Beth raised her eyes she found Nanny Gwyn's upon her and the old lady nodded before saying, "You have questions, I know, Miss Watson, so why don't you begin with the first one. . ."

Beth was grateful to be given this opening, but now that the moment had arrived she felt a twinge of apprehension and stirred her tea slowly by way of distraction.

"Thank you. . . Nanny," the name sounded odd to her ears for she had never had cause to call anyone by that title, but the old lady was so candid and accommodating Beth was sure she would grow accustomed to it in time. "The child, my charge; forgive me, but I do not recall her name being mentioned during the meeting earlier with the master, indeed. . ." she lowered her eyes, "if I am to be truthful, I have not been acquainted with her name at all."

There was a long pause before the old lady spoke, and when she did her words were underlined with a profound sadness.

"Ah Miss Watson, I can see that you are as shrewd as you are sensible and you are right, of course. I'm afraid that the name of the child is as controversial as is her presence in the house. I will explain more fully so you will gain a better understanding, but first know that her name as was given to her is Eleri."

"Eleri. . ." breathed Beth softly. At last! Her charge had ownership of a proper identity. A status. A name!

"But," said Nanny Gwyn with just a hint of disapproval in the soft Welsh tones, "We do not call her by the name with which she was baptised with; indeed it is forbidden. The master requires that she be known as Emily." She shifted in the chair and looked to the flames as they danced and flickered, "It is the only thing we disagree upon. But it is at the insistence of the mistress that she be addressed as Emily, and so for the sake of compromise the master felt he had little choice other than to agree. . ." She pursed her lips and Beth stared at her openly perplexed.

What did she mean at the insistence of the mistress?

Nanny Gwyn turned and faced her and there was a flush to her cheeks that wasn't entirely from the warmth of the fire. In a tight voice she continued;

"It is because of the scandal, you see. The mistress is keen to distance herself and the family from the child and the circumstances of her birth. Indeed if the mistress had had her way the child would never have come into the house! But the master, for once, stood his ground and. . . well. . . he got his way in the end, but the conditions are such that the child's natural name must not be spoken, and that. . ." the old woman paused and Beth saw a sudden glint come into the usually kind eyes, "her presence in the house is to be contained at all times and be. . . discreet."

Hidden away more like, thought Beth indignantly and was shocked at the cruelty of it. That this poor orphaned child should be punished for the sins of the mother as if losing her and then finding herself cast adrift in the world was not enough! But then to be forbidden the very name that had been bestowed on her from birth was almost too much to bear, so harsh was the directive, so... unnecessary.

Beth could see that beneath Nanny Gwyn's composure she was as unhappy about it as she was. But for all of her elevated status she was still only a servant, and if the master was weak as she was clearly implying he was, then it was the mistress who was the real power of the house and besides; the old lady had not been *her* nanny. . .

It was an unsettling and disturbing development and explained why the family children took their meals and their lessons in the main part of the house. There was a clear demarcation line and a deliberate act of isolation against an innocent child, and Beth was now keener than ever to meet with this unwanted scrap of humanity.

She leaned forward.

"May I see her?"

"She will be asleep now. She sleeps a lot. Perhaps it would be better to wait until the morning, Miss Watson. You are of the same heart and mind as I am, I can see that, but there are still things you need to know and so I would advise patience, for tomorrow will come soon enough." Nanny said gently. "As I mentioned, I am not in favour of this change of name and I will confess there are times when I forget," she gave Beth a direct look, "and so often, and to avoid dispute, it is easier for me, and for the master to refrain from using her name at all. . .unless we are in the vicinity of the mistress, of course."

"Oh but this is so terribly sad, and so, so. . ." began Beth and Nanny Gwyn silenced her with a finger to her lips.

"It is what it is, Miss Watson, and beware, for the walls have ears. Take heart that we do the best we can, the master and myself. But just so you are aware the child is not permitted into the main living quarters, but you can visit the gardens with her and access is allowed via the great hall if there are no guests and the family is not about. These are the conditions, and if you are to remain here, and I do so hope you will, be sure to adhere to them for the sake of the child if nothing else." She reached down and pulling a log out from the box threw it on to the fire, "the few who have come before you left, or were dismissed, for their failure to abide by the rules. It is a hard task, I know, but by being discreet and working together, it is my fervent hope that we can provide some stability and much-needed comfort without cause for...complaint."

There was a prolonged silence as the two women regarded each other. Beth understood precisely what it was the old retainer was suggesting and there was an acknowledgment of this in her eyes. In contrast Nanny Gwyn's were hooded but there passed between them a complicit comprehension and Beth could not help but thrill to this unprecedented situation.

"I am happy to be guided by your wisdom and experience and wish only the best for the child," she said quietly, and the old woman nodded before turning back to the fire a small smile playing upon her lips.

"Thank you, Miss Watson; I knew I could rely on you. And now, I must apprise you of the events surrounding the child and how she came to being, and for that we must go back to when a harpist called Gwydion ap Dewi came to Galinas House to play one Christmas..."

Beth took a sip of her tea and waited.

"He was a bard from Ynys Mon and a handsome one at that! Claimed descent from the druids that once flourished on the Island and he was certainly charismatic enough. He recited and played beautifully, and Margaret, the master's sister was enchanted on the spot. There were other entertainers, of course, but none to compare with the magic of this poor humble musician with his handsome looks and dark flashing eyes. And so when the festivities were over, Margaret, determined to see him again, prevailed upon her brother that he be given a place in the house so that she could learn to play the harp; and he, who could deny his beloved sister nothing, agreed."

Nanny shook her head sadly.

"They say love can strike you blind, and it wasn't just Margaret who was afflicted, because the master, in the goodness of his nature and wanting only to please, did not see the look in his sister's eyes nor did he the danger of a young woman in the throes of her first love, and he blames himself, I know, for enabling the lovers to submit to their passion; and under his own roof, no less! But that was only the beginning. . ." she broke off and looked across to where Beth sat spellbound so much so she could hardly breathe, and there was genuine pain in the old lady's eyes.

"She was such a beautiful girl, Margaret; as dainty as a Welsh fairy but with a strong will, unlike her brother. And when she came of age she no less headstrong and was renowned throughout the county for her beauty and. . . Forgive me, Miss Watson, but I feel compelled to be completely honest with you for I sense integrity in you that I can trust and besides, if you are to fully understand the circumstances in which you find yourself, I can be nothing less than forthright. I hope you understand. . ."

"I do." Beth's voice was little more than a whisper. She had been in anticipation of being privy to a family scandal but this was turning into a sorrowful and troubling tale.

"Well the inevitable happened, of course, and soon Margaret was with child. She came to me in confidence, distraught at her predicament, but there was nothing else for it than throw herself on her brother's mercy. He was shocked, naturally, but so great was his love for her he was willing to be nothing less than generous. But as soon as the mistress was informed she flew into a terrible rage and insisted they both be banished from the house, that she would not suffer such sin under her roof! It was a terrible scene."

"They?" questioned Beth.

"Oh yes," said Nanny, "unlike many who would have fled and left her to her fate, the harpist remained true for they were deeply in love, Miss Watson, this was no light affair of the heart. They were committed to each other, so much so, that when the master cast them out they packed their belongings and left for a new life near the coast where they lived simply but happily, and then disaster struck."

Nanny Gwyn gave Beth an earnest look.

"I remained in touch with her, you see; secretly. There could be no other way. Tegid took care of the messages that went back and fore, God bless him, and at times I sent money when work was scarce for him, for life as a musical bard is hard and erratic and they lacked much, I know." She sighed and shook her head. "You cannot raise a child from the cradle and stop loving them even when they have committed so great a sin and moved miles beyond all sight and knowing, and Lord knows I loved her like my own."

There were tears beaded in the old lady's eyes as she gazed back into the fire and Beth felt her sadness like a breath of dying air.

"One stormy night when no man had any business being on the sea, Gwydion went down on a boat that was crossing the Menai Strait. He was returning home with some fellow musicians after playing at a wedding party in Beaumaris. Couldn't wait until the sea had calmed, would not take the advice of his fellow companions, declared he had done that crossing so many times that his ancestors watched over him and would ensure his protection. Somehow, and only the good Lord knows how, he managed to persuade a boatman to cast off and make the trip, so keen was he to return to his family, for Margaret was with child again and did not like to alone, But his impatience was his undoing and his ancestors must have been looking the other way that night, for the boat was swept onto the rocks where both he and the poor boatman perished."

Beth drew in a deep breath as Nanny Gwyn fell silent for some moments. Shadows from the fire leaped and danced round the room and somewhere on the moors an owl gave a long drawn-out cry.

"Margaret had been out on the cliffs keeping watch on the other side. Some said that she slipped; others reckoned the sight of seeing the man she loved go to his death unhinged her and that she threw herself down on to the rocks below." She shook her head slowly, "I don't suppose we'll ever know, as we will not the devastating effect this had on Eleri when she woke the next morning only to find that she was alone and that her mother was nowhere to be seen. . . Lord knows there are some things a child should not see for it was Eleri who found her mother on the rocks. And such was the shock she screamed like a stricken beast until the neighbours sent for the doctor who had to sedate her; they could not stop the screaming, you see, and that was the last time anyone heard a sound out of that poor child's lips."

Nanny Gwyn's eyes reflected the tragedy of the whole story as she turned back to Beth who now sat shocked and ramrod straight.

"That was just over a twelve month ago, and it is my belief that the child is nothing more than an empty husk with no more will to live than anyone who has been brought down by the deepest pain. And so you see our predicament, Miss Watson, the circumstances, the aftermath, the whole sorry tale and how we flounder like fish on a rock for there is nothing that we've tried, or haven't tried, to bring this child back from the darkness into which she has put herself." Sniffing she pulled a hanky from her skirt pocket and dabbed away the tears as Beth found herself swallowing back a few of her own.

"Oh. . . Nanny Gwyn," she murmured sadly, "I. . . I don't really know what to say. . ."

"What is there to say? Other than we must do our best as we can for the child. . . for Eleri," said Nanny and her tone softened as she said the name. "The master can do no more than he has done, and the mistress would have him do less if she could and so it is a delicate situation that has been beyond the power of any of us thus far. We endeavour, Miss Watson, but it is an uphill journey I fear will see me into an early grave such is the sorrow of it."

Impulsively Beth went across and knelt before the old lady and taking her hands in hers fixed her a look that was as vehement as it was tender.

"Then let me take up the burden of it; all of it!" she said with a fierceness that surprised her and she saw Nanny's eyes widen "Tell me, show me all there is to know and allow yourself the time to step back, to rest, to draw breath; it has been a truly dreadful time that would take its toll on anyone and I want to help you so much! Both of you and so I will, you'll see!"

"Why, *Bach*," said Nanny Gwyn and through the tears she gave a tremulous smile, "so young, so full of spirit; you fill me with such hope that I dare not think of it! I knew it, when I saw you. I felt it my bones, and hope is not something that lives easily in this house. . ."

Another shade of sadness passed over her eyes.

"What? What is it?" urged Beth, "if there is more, please you can trust me, I promise you!"

"No, it's nothing. Just the ramblings of a silly old woman," she said and gave Beth's hands a small squeeze. "I'm just so thankful that you've come, as is the master, for doubt not that he cares greatly for the child and he grieves still for her mother, I know, and curses himself oftimes for the day he ever allowed Gwydion ap Dewi into this house!"

"What of his family, Nanny Gwyn? They must know of Eleri surely; what part have they played in all this?"

"Very little, I'm sad to say. They are poor, Miss Watson, good, honest folk but poor. They had given everything so that Gwydion could pursue his dream and their love has cost them dearly. Such is their grief at losing their only son they have turned their faces away."

Beth withdrew her hands and knelt back pained disbelief evident in her eyes.

"Yes, I know, but often such is the case when ill-fated love brings a child into the world. We live in harsh and cruel times, Miss Watson, where the only protection is power and position, and if you haven't got that then it is not unlike the fickleness of the sea that took poor Gwydion that night. And so we sail and we swim through it with the best that God gave us, but take heart. . ." she leaned forward, "for we, at least, are in such a position that we can assist the child and help weather the storms that rage around her, can we not?"

Beth nodded.

"Then let that be our pact. Trust no one in this house, Miss Watson, seek only advice from me for there are eyes and ears everywhere and I am afraid you will be watched."

"Watched?" Beth hadn't thought she could be any more surprised.

"Miss Meacham, the governess; be careful what you say around her and be sure to take the greatest care when you are with Eleri. I have known for some time that she reports back to the mistress. It is all part of how she accrues favour and privileges, and also be aware of the mischief of children, for I am sad to say, having also been their nurse, that with the exception of the youngest, the other two are their mother's children." she gave Beth a keen look, "You understand what it is I am telling you, Miss Watson?"

"Yes," said Beth quietly.

"Then may you stay long with us and prosper, Miss Watson, for Lord knows things cannot go on much longer as they are. . . "

Chapter 4

The next morning dawned bright and sunny as the mist rippled away reluctantly before a brisk wind. Beth sat in the window seat and took in the miles of rugged heath beneath a cloudless sky and couldn't help but marvel at the vastness of it. Having risen early after a fragmented night of snatched sleep and strange dreams, she'd washed and dressed but there was little appetite for the breakfast tray that Gwen had brought her and it sat barely touched on the side table.

She was far too restless for that.

Her thoughts were all for the child and the terrible plight in which she'd found herself, and how the previous night Nanny Gwyn had thrown all caution to the wind and in desperation had confided in her. That the old nurse was at the end of her tether was clearly evident, despite her initial air of composure. Embroiled amidst a divided family; torn between love and loyalty, and, most bizarrely of all, forbidden to give voice to the child's real name. Beth could only wonder at what manner of woman the mistress could be to be so blatantly unjust to a small, defenceless child, and as she heard the long-awaited tap at the door, she rose with expectant relief.

Nanny. At last! She had come, as she said she would, to collect Beth and take her for her first meeting with little Eleri.

"Please come in!" she called and the smile died on her lips as the door opened and a tall woman of middling age came in and fixed her with a haughty stare.

"Oh!" uttered Beth in surprise, "I beg your pardon, I was expecting Nanny Gwyn."

"So it would seem," replied the woman and arched her eyebrows that were light and sandy as the hair that was scraped severely back into a bun. She was dressed in a dark brown gown that did little to lift the pallor of her skin as she regarded Beth out of slightly protruding eyes of a pale, nondescript colour.

"I am Miss Meacham, the children's governess. The mistress wishes to meet with you before you see the child."

Her manner was chilled and unfriendly, the tone grand, and Beth saw in the eyes a snake-like slyness and inwardly she thanked Nanny Gwyn for warning her of this woman. With a pleasant smile she rose to her feet.

"Why, thank you, Miss Meacham, I am pleased to make your acquaintance." She went forward and held out her hand. The governess took it with the greatest of reluctance and gave it the briefest of shakes.

"Follow me, please."

Beth hesitated and the tall woman paused giving her a questioning look.

"Nanny Gwyn, she . . ."

Again Miss Meacham raised the finely arched eyebrows.

"Well, will she not wonder where I've gone? She said to. . ."

"Miss Watson!" the governess cut in frostily, "There is but one mistress here and it not Nanny Gwyn; you may do well to remember that!"

Beth bowed her head realising she had made her first mistake and her heart plummeted in dismay. This didn't bode well and she knew she needed be even more careful now she was about to be brought before the mistress.

Soon they were in the heart of the house where the family lived but it still retained the inherent gloominess despite the grand furnishings and portraits along the walls. The governess led the way to the far end of the house and she stopped before a door at the end. Turning to Beth she said in a low voice.

"The mistress is having one of her better mornings, but just be aware that she tires easily and has no patience for. . . *prattle*"

She bestowed upon Beth a thinly-veiled look of spite as though to imply that Beth possessed this particular trait, and inwardly the young woman bristled but held her peace.

"Miss Watson, my lady."

As she followed Miss Meacham into a plushly-appointed room she was struck at first by how dim it was in there. The heavy drapes across the windows were barely open, and she could just make out a figure reclining on a chaise lounge who watched her approach with the air of a cat intent upon a mouse.

"Stand there," said Miss Meacham curtly.

Beth stood in the corridor of light that came from the nearest window and waited. The air was full and stuffy relieved only by a strong smell of rose-water. The governess had gone to stand near the recumbent figure and several seconds ticked by before the mistress of the house deigned to speak.

"Why, what an attractive young woman you are, Miss Watson! Not quite what I expected. . . not quite what I expected at all. . ."

She left the statement linger in the air for a moment as though to suggest this could be an issue but Beth did not change expression and maintained a respectful silence.

"Not that it matters," the languorous voice went on, "for you have come, as have many have before you, to assist with an impossible task that is a folly in itself, and no doubt you will fail, as they all have. . . come closer."

Beth stepped forward obediently and as her eyes adjusted to the gloom she took her first look at her charge's nemesis and the mistress of the house.

Swathed in a loosely-held gown, she was a voluptuous woman who once would've been deemed becoming before ill-health and the resultant lassitude had claimed her. The eyes were still fine, and her hair, coiled in a loose chignon retained traces of its former Titian splendour, but there was a petulance about the small mouth and the green eyes now sparkled maliciously as they took in Beth's cool beauty and calm demeanour.

"Your father was a man of the cloth, was he not? And your mother, one-time lady's maid to Lady Foley, I believe."

"Yes, m'am." Said Beth quietly. She felt uncomfortable under the emerald stare and wondered what was coming next.

The mistress nodded as though satisfied that Beth's background in some way passed muster.

"And so you are well versed in godliness, one would hope, Miss Watson; especially with such. . . looks. . ."

Beth felt her cheeks redden under the barely-concealed insult as Miss Meacham's narrow face twitched with amusement.

"For know that I will have no light behaviour in my house, nor shall I suffer any breach of house rules; but then I expect you have been well instructed in the etiquette of service courtesy of your mother?"

"Yes, m'am, indeed, I have."

"Good. Then you will also know that although I am frequently indisposed, I am kept well informed nevertheless, and the children," her plump features softened for a moment, "must not have any more disruption than they have had to endure, and so for the sake of their protection, your contact with them shall be minimal. Do I make myself understood?"

Beth dipped her head, and then the mistress suddenly seemed to lose interest and lay back murmuring, "I have a headache coming on, Meacham, a nice massage with some oils would be most beneficial, I feel. This whole business is just so. . . tiresome. See Miss Watson out, would you."

The governess glided out from behind her mistress like a ghoul relieved of its watch and holding the door open gave a terse nod as Beth passed her, relieved to be dismissed. Contrary to what Miss Meacham had implied, it had been a much shorter interview than she'd anticipated and she walked quickly from the family quarters and back to her own.

Nanny Gwyn was sat in the window seat waiting for her, and Beth smiled widely, delighted to see a friendly face.

"Oh Nanny, I'm so sorry, but Miss Meacham. . ."

Nanny held up a hand, "There is no need to apologise, Miss Watson, I had an inkling you might have been summoned." She took in Beth's flushed cheeks and nodded knowingly.

"Acquainted herself with you, did she?"

Beth drew a deep breath and rolled her eyes comically as Nanny suppressed a smile.

"And Miss Meacham?"

"Oh yes. . ." said Beth, "and I don't mind saying that I'm glad it is over! I thought for one moment I was going to be dismissed on the spot!"

"It's just the Mistress's way of asserting her authority, although she doesn't usually summon the new nurse for inspection *quite* so soon. I can only assume you made a good impression with the master and she would've been curious, is all, but no matter. I've taken the child down into the garden for some air; such a fine day cannot be wasted! Gwen is sat out with her at present but it is time, methinks, Miss Watson, for you to finally make her acquaintance!"

"Why, with pleasure, Nanny, please lead on!"

With a sense of excitement Beth followed the old lady as she took the back stairs that led out to a small walled garden.

Along the gravelled path a small figure sat hunched on one of the stone benches like an abandoned sprite left behind by the fairies. Even from this distance Beth could see the air of sadness around her that she wore like a heavy cloak. Gwen was sat beside her and appeared to be talking animatedly with much waving of the hands, but the little figure remained motionless and Beth's heart reached out to her.

The maid stood as she saw them approach and dipped a small curtsey.

"Thank you, Gwen," said Nanny.

She waited until she had returned to the house before moving round to where the maid had been sat and indicated that Beth stay back for a moment.

"*Cariad bach*," she said softly, "There is someone here to see you. . . a nice young woman, a *kind* young woman, and she has come all the way from a little market town called Brecon just to be with you!" she leaned in and whispered something in the young girl's ear.

Beth waited quietly as the sun shone brightly warming the back of her neck and somewhere just over the way she heard a horse whinny in greeting and wondered if the stables were nearby.

Nanny was beckoning to her and moving forward Beth brought herself round until she was stood in front of the huddled figure and in one graceful movement bent down before the small dark head.

The child kept her eyes lowered as Beth looked into a wan little face that was as closed and as shuttered as surely as if a blind had been pulled down. The delicate brows and eyelashes were as dark as her hair that had been tied back with a blue ribbon; and the lips were like a tiny bow as though pursed in thoughtful consideration. A fine sprinkling of freckles tried valiantly to add colour to the ghostly pallor and the young woman believed it was the saddest face she ever saw.

Reaching out and with great gentleness she reached out her hands and took the child's fingers in her own. Despite the warm sunlight there was a chill within them and Beth folded them into hers all but willing some life into them.

"Eleri. . ." she said in a tone so hushed it was like the merest whisper, "my name is Beth, and I have come to help you if you'll let me."

The child remained unmoving, but Beth had a sense she was listening. "I'm so sorry about your mam and da. . ." she went on slipping unconsciously back into childhood language, "I know you have lost the two most precious beings in the world and I cannot even begin to know how sad you are feeling. But I lost my da some years ago. . . and so can understand a little bit."

The lips twitched just ever so slightly as Beth, her voice low and mellifluous kept her eyes on the little face, "I have always wanted a little sister, but there were no more children after I came. I always thought it would be nice to have someone to confide in. . . to share my secrets with. . . to braid my hair and help choose ribbons and well, just to be there with me as a friend, too, when I'm feeling sad" She gave the small fingers the tiniest squeeze, "So I could be like a big sister to *you*, if that pleases you, Eleri. . . someone you can trust, like Nanny Gwyn, someone to be your friend only like a sister to look out for you. . .*watch over you*. . ."

She emphasized the last words and paused for some moments before being rewarded as with a faint flutter the eyelashes slowly rose to reveal the deepest, darkest, most tragic eyes Beth had ever seen, and there flickered in the sable depths just the merest movement before the lids drew down and the lashes stilled once more upon the porcelain skin.

Beth glanced up at Nanny Gwyn her face wreathed in disbelief and the old nurse mirrored her expression as she clasped her hands ecstatically, and then rising from her seat she indicated that Beth take her place.

"Why, what a lovely morning it is turning out to be and as the sun is most kind on these old bones of mine, I'm going to take a little stroll in it and enjoy God's blessing!" she announced and there was barely suppressed excitement in her voice. Her eyes were shining as they beamed her delight at this unexpected breakthrough, and determined not to let the moment pass she nodded vigorously at Beth before moving away.

The young woman was at a loss as to what she could say other than something about herself, and so as the bees buzzed and birds trilled about them Beth simply sat and held the Eleri's hand as she spoke about her life and her family; about the noisy mills of Newport, how relieved she and her mother took her to live in the green hills of Brecon. About her Taid's dog, *Seren* and how her Nain could bring a room to tears with her singing. She spoke of happy things and fond recollections, and although Eleri made no response, the chill left her hand as Beth's warmth and vitality gradually breached the gap and the young woman knew that she was listening.

By the time Nanny Gwyn came back into view the two were sat in a strange but comfortable silence. The child's shoulders had slightly lifted and Beth had her face to the sun. The old nurse shook her head amazed at this remarkable development.

That there had been some kind of connection made between them, she had no doubt and for the first time since Eleri had come into the house, she harboured hope in her heart but as yet would say nothing to the master. It was still early days, but it was an encouraging start as it was wholly unexpected, and as she reached the two figures on the bench she held out a small posy of white flowers to Beth.

"For your room," she said smiling, "they're from the Hawthorn tree and are known to have various properties,"

Beth realised that a gift of sorts was being given and she took the flowers gratefully.

"Thank you, Nanny," she said quietly, "I will find a place for them next to my bed."

Nanny nodded and then gave a small clap of her hands.

"Why, it's nearly time for luncheon! And here are we chattering like a bunch of magpies when Cook has said she would make us her special flan! I hope you are feeling hungry after your time in the fresh air, *cariad*, and maybe you are ready to partake of a nice glass of milk?"

She addressed the question to the child without expecting an answer and reaching down took Eleri's other hand as Beth rose from the seat still holding the other one.

With the ease of compliance the child came to her feet and then walked slowly between them her head carried low, but there was a hint of pink in the paleness of the cheeks and like Nanny Gwyn, Beth dared to hope the impossible. Yet she had heard and learned enough to know that the herculean task before her would be evenly matched by the hostilities she would have to face within the house.

Now she could understand Tegid's warning and Nanny's concerns, and yet in spite of it all she found her resolve quickening like the wings of a bird before flight as inwardly she gathered herself for the fight ahead.

Chapter 5

The next few days fell into a kind of pattern as Beth was as true as her word and took more duties upon herself in the care of the child. Now instead of Nanny breaking fast with Eleri in the nursery, Beth took her place as she did all other tasks and in a calm, competent manner, and although there had been no further interest shown by Eleri as to her new carer and routine, there was no resistance either, and an ambience of cautious relaxation began to permeate that part of the upper house.

The days were spent with Beth invariably reading stories and maintaining a steady line of idle chatter. And often, weather permitting; Beth would lead Eleri down to the garden after luncheon where sometimes they would just sit amidst the heady scent of the flowers as a sunny breeze breathed over them and birdsong accompanied them.

During these times Nanny Gwyn would take a nap and was grateful to be doing so, as Beth quietly assumed sole charge of the little girl in a way that was both practical and sensitive. Beth was careful to keep herself and her charge in their part of the house, and to be heard addressing her charge as Emily on the two occasions Miss Meacham had visited the nursery on the pretext of wanting some pencils.

As yet she had not encountered the Squire's children but she had heard them, the boy especially, when their voices floated across from the stables that were close to the gardens, and she often thought it sad that Eleri was denied the company of her cousins but she did not dare flout the rules and was always careful to ensure their paths didn't cross.

Old Tegid had been as good as his word and the Squire had agreed that Beth could have use of an old brood mare on her day off, and when Nanny had informed her of this Beth's eyes shone with delight for she was keen to explore the local area and acquaint herself with the nearest village. "I think the master would happily let you ride his best hunter, if it was up to him!" said Nanny Gwyn as she poured the tea. "So pleased is he with you! And I have to say that the child is looking better. Not speaking still, granted, but she *looks* better, and when Dr. Morgan comes to call next week he will also be well pleased to see the change in her, I know."

Beth settled back into one of Nanny's chairs and gave a contented sigh. Eleri was taking her usual nap late in the afternoon which gave the two women time to catch up on their charge's progress and discuss ideas of how else they may inveigle the child out from her silence.

Beth always enjoyed these times and the comforting presence of Nanny Gwyn. For the most part her day was spent so focused on Eleri and thinking up new ways of diversion, that it was only when she stopped that she realised how draining it could become, and she marvelled that the old nurse had managed for as long as she did.

The two women had developed a trust and an accord between them forged by their love for the child, for, as Beth had written to her mother, how could one not! Her Eleri *bach* as she called her was like an injured fawn that had turned its face from the world and Beth was unbridled in her determination to bring her back.

Just be mindful, her mother had written back, *for there were few things more powerful in the house than a servant who had the ear of the master, and the fact it was the mistress in this case, made it no less dangerous,* she warned. *But I am delighted as well*; she had added *that you have found your place and have such good terms with the old nurse. Alliances between staff can make or break a person's position – particularly when you are young and inexperienced, and so be sure to pass on my gratitude and best wishes to Mrs Gwyn.*

As Nanny chattered away Beth suddenly had a thought, and sitting forward cried, "Oh Nanny, why did I not think of it before!"

The old lady broke off and looked at her in surprise.

"Why, the stables, no, no, I mean the *horses!* Gwen mentioned the other day that a foal had been born and that she is the sweetest thing! Can we not visit and meet the new arrival? Oh please say we can, Nanny that would be permitted, surely!"

"Well, I don't see why not. . ... and I don't suppose Tegid would mind," said Nanny thoughtfully, "in fact, the more I think about it, the more it appeals, for the day a child isn't moved by something as special as a newborn would be a sorry day indeed! Leave it with me, I think it is a splendid idea, but let it be just you and Eleri, for if the experience may unlock her in some way, and if it does, God willing, let you be the first to have that pleasure!"

"But. . ."

"No, buts," said the old nurse firmly, "you have taken on this task and the child with such commitment I would not have it any other way. Now then, *Cariad*, what about some *cacen* with this tea?"

As Beth took a slice of fruit loaf from the proffered plate another question rose to her lips but she hesitated for she was unsure as to how it would be received. That Nanny Gwyn was kind and canny, she had no doubt, but the old nurse had also been through much with Eleri and the shift in the household and so would it be fair? Had she not been given enough to deal with?

The young woman decided to keep her peace, but she was troubled.

There had been things going on in her room; *unexplained* things. . .

Items had moved from place to place. Objects going missing, and then turning up. She recalled her first night in the house when Nanny had come by to collect her for dinner. She had been reading in the window seat and had put the book on the bedside table before leaving the room. And yet upon her return; the book was on the bed.

At the time she dismissed the incident with the explanation that perhaps she *thought* she had placed the book next to the bed; it had been a long day, she was tired, there had been a lot to take in. But then she woke one morning to find her hairbrush next to her pillow, and one afternoon, upon slipping into her room for a shawl she discovered that the flowers Nanny had given her were strewn across the floor, and yet the simple vase they had been sat in remained upright on the dressing table!

These incidents were as disconcerting as they were random, and she suspected they were being committed deliberately in a bid to frighten her. She had been warned to take care of unfriendly influences in the house, had she not? By both Nanny Gwyn and the head stableman, not to mention by the Squire's wife herself! And yet, who would do such a thing? And who would have the audacity to actually *come into her bedchamber* whilst she slept!

Admittedly her first thought was Miss Meacham, but the idea of the straight-backed governess stooping to anything so low was dismissed almost as soon as it came, for her inflated sense of importance would never allow it.

But what was to stop her, especially if it was at the mistress's directive, to impinge on a lesser member of staff who would have very little choice other than to obey.

As Nanny poured more tea and reminisced of days gone by, Beth drew up the list of likely suspects she had mentally compiled amongst the serving maids. Gwen she had removed from it immediately; the girl was helpful and friendly, but then hadn't Nanny specifically warned her to trust no one else in the house?

Beth ruminated furiously. No, she could believe it of the cheery red-haired little maid, she had been so kind to Beth; nothing was too much trouble, but she did inwardly look askance at the mouse-like Mary who sometimes made up her fire, or another girl called Non who had sly eyes and a sullen manner.

If it was to be anyone, she decided, it would be one of the last two, and she resolved not to betray, by as much as a look or a change in her demeanour that she knew, but she would become more vigilant and in a sudden bloom of light had the thinking she would set a trap!

The thought excited her as it also disturbed her that she should be reduced to such a course of action, but then someone was entering her room when she wasn't there, and on for occasion when she was asleep! And surely the Squire would not condone such malicious activity whether it was under his wife's instruction or not?

The prim face of the governess rose in her mind like a disapproving ghost and Beth's certainty grew. That she was jealous of her, she knew. But then Miss Meacham's lot was hardly a happy one; plain of disposition, penurious in her circumstances, and attached, unwilling or otherwise, to a household that a stronger bloodline or fate may have seen herself the mistress of.

Small wonder she clung to her dignity like a ragged cloak, and such fragility of her position would ensure that anyone she perceived as having any form of influence would be regarded as nothing less than a threat.

I will place something in the door the next time I leave the room, she thought, like a strand of my cotton. And at night something a bit more robust that will awaken me as soon as someone comes in. The idea satisfied her. She was loathe to bother Nanny with it as yet, and besides, it would take more than that to scare me her away from her position and Eleri *bach,* she told herself.

She brought her attention fully back to Nanny who was now enquiring something of her.

"Suitable attire? Why, yes, Nanny, my mother made some alterations and has given me her old riding habit. Just in case there was an opportunity; although I'm not actually that experienced."

"Just mention that to Tegid, I'm sure he will reassure you that the mare that's been chosen will be suitable and if she isn't, then Lord knows they have nearly as many horses in those stables as they have servants!"

And so when Beth made her way somewhat nervously to the stables on her first free day, the old man met her in the yard with a warm smile and a sturdy Welsh cob.

"This is Hefina," he said stroking the proud neck, "she's an old brood mare and you'll not find a steadier or a sweeter girl from here to the Llyn Peninsula! She'll take good care of you, Miss, I can promise you that."

Beth looked at the chestnut mare with her flaxen mane and was immediately soothed by the softness in the eyes that regarded her calmly. Tentatively she held out a slice of apple she'd brought for the occasion and the lips puckered before taking the treat gently.

"A good start there, Miss, I have to say, now come in closer and say a proper hello," As he stepped back holding the reins loosely, Beth came forward and allowed the mare to sniff her hands before she stroked the soft muzzle.

"There! Friends already!" the head stableman nodded his head to the young boy as he worked the water pump into a line of buckets. "Steffan there can accompany you out, if you would like, Miss, since it's your first time out on the moors .. ?"

Beth looked at the old man gratefully.

"Thank you, *diolch*, that's so kind, but I intend only to ride to the village which, as Nanny informed me, is just a few miles away and signposted well and I would rather be alone."

Tegid took his well-used pipe out from an inner pocket and pretended to inspect the empty bowl.

"Well if you're sure, Miss. Just be aware that mists can come down suddenly on these moors and well, we wouldn't want you getting lost, now would we? Not now that we've found you! I hear you're doing well in the post, Miss, very well indeed," he nodded his head with evident pleasure adding, "Nan also mentioned you'd like to bring the child for a visit, so know that you are both welcome to come anytime and that the new foal is a beauty, four perfect white socks! Horses are healing creatures, Miss Watson, and for want of a more humble opinion, I declare myself in favour of what benefit the child may derive from such an encounter. Just send word when you're ready. . . Now then! How like you your new friend, Hefina, Miss?"

"I like her more than well. Thank you, she's perfect!"

"Then let you both be better acquainted," And without further ado he led the mare across to the mounting block.

As Beth settled herself into the side-saddle and adjusted her skirts, she could not help but feel a rising tide of excitement at the anticipation of a few hours to herself and a chance to explore the area. It had been a busy time since she'd arrived and with so much to preoccupy her, a couple of hours in the saddle on such a beautiful day would be like a tonic to her spirits.

With a kindly shake of her head she refused Tegid's offer again of taking one of the grooms.

"Aye, well, I can't say I blame you wanting some time away on your own," he said as he checked the girths, "just be mindful of the mists. They can come down suddenly and the moors are vast and can be treacherous." He stood back and looked up at her. "Straight out from the yard, Miss, and where the track forks, take the right. Make sure you stay on the path."

As Beth came out from the yard on to the heath she breathed deeply and duly took the path to the right. Soon she and Hefina were plodding along both at ease with each other and as clouds scudded across the blue skies chivvied along by a brisk breeze, for the first time since coming to the House Beth felt as though she could relax.

The path was wide and smoothed by years of passage, and as soon as the young woman became accustomed to the saddle, she took up the pace and urged the mare into an easy trot that soon went into an easy canter and before she knew it a sprawl of cottages came into sight; they had reached the village.

It was bigger than she had expected and bustling with people going about their work. A steady clanging came from the blacksmith's and two women sat weaving baskets ceased in their chatter to watch Beth pass by. There were two inns, a small schoolhouse, and a lovely old church that sat back from the main street. Her presence was beginning to cause quite a slight stir as people now regarded Beth with open curiosity but she knew it was because her face was a strange one and that they probably surmised she was from the great house and probably knew who she was.

She continued on through the village and coming out the other end decided not to return through the speculative stares and took a path that would bring her round and back up on to the moors.

With just the wind and the cry of a skylark as it soared in flight Beth felt an uncharacteristic need to take her few hours of freedom to new heights and loosening her riding bonnet she urged Hefina to go faster, and soon they were flying across the moors as Beth's hair came loose and her bonnet went spinning. She laughed with euphoria as she imagined Miss Meacham's face if she could see her now, but the constraints of living in such a tense environment had obviously taken its toll and she laughed afresh caught up in the moment.

The ground had risen slightly and as they went over the other side, Beth heard gurgling water, and guiding her mount to its source they soon came upon a spring and the horse dipped her head to it eagerly.

"Ah Hefina, good girl! What a wonderful girl you are! Why, I think you enjoyed that as much as me!" gasped Beth gleefully, and she relaxed in the saddle as Hefina drank her fill as she tried and failed to re-pin her hair. "Oh dear," she said, "What a sight I will look on our return, *and* minus my hat!"

Coiling her hair into some kind of knot shrugged she gathered up the reins as Hefina stepped back from the spring and then turning her round drew her breath sharply in dismay.

A bank of mist was rolling in like a living thing, thin grey fingers questing, and she felt her heart plummet as all carefree laughter and madness of the moment disappeared in an instant.

The old mare pawed the rough ground and let loose a heavy snort.

"Ah well, Hefina, let's pray you know the moors well enough and can lead us home, for I have no idea!" she leaned forward and patted the mare's neck and then proceeded back the way they'd come and into the mist.

As horse and rider moved cautiously through the damp murk, Beth realised in hindsight why the old man had been so concerned for the mist had literally descended and crept in behind her, and she resolved to make a humble apology the minute she returned – if she ever did, for the greyness had become almost tangible so thick was it now, the sun little more than a faint halo.

It was some time before they found the path, but find it they did, and Beth was so relieved she could have wept.

But which way?

She'd lost all sense of direction and was now seriously concerned for who was to say she was on the *right* path! There had been many tributaries leading off, some more well-used than others and she scolded herself for her foolishness before being struck by an idea so logical, it seemed ridiculous! She would let Hefina find the way home! Why, of course! Horses were known for it, were they not? The lure of a warm stable, a handful of oats! And so without further ado she released the reins and made a clicking sound and Hefina pricked up her ears.

"Come on then, girl. lead the way home. I know you can do it!" she whispered, and with a relaxed gait the mare began moving forward and once again Beth was overcome with relief.

Nothing moved in the mist. No sounds. No birdsong. It was as though they were completely alone in the world, and then she heard a jingle of harness in the distance and glimpsed faint movement as a horse and rider gradually came into view.

A man's voice said, "Whoaaaa . ." and from the mist appeared a smartly-dressed man atop a long-legged bay. Together they slowed down from a steady jog and pulled up at the sight of Beth as she, too, drew Hefina to a halt.

"Hello, are you lost?"

Any apprehension Beth may have been harbouring at meeting a stranger on the road dissipated at the sound of his tone. Polite, educated, and flavoured with the local accent.

"Yes, I'm afraid I am," she replied in embarrassment, "I was given fair warning about the mist and foolishly I heeded it not. Please, can you tell me if I am on the right road for Galinas House?"

The man came forward and she saw a handsome face that peered at her intensely with a slight frown.

"Why yes, you are on the right road but are going the wrong way. Have you met with an accident of some kind? Your hair..?"

"No, no!" said Beth and raised one hand to her tumbling tresses self-consciously as she realised that her bun had come loose, the pins somewhere on the moors along with her hat.

"I lost my bonnet, the wind was. . . stronger than I thought and I hadn't tied . . ." she trailed off and hoped that the grey light spared him the sight of her flushed cheeks, so great was her embarrassment.

The man's lips twitched beneath his dark moustache and losing his frown he held out a hand and introduced himself.

"Emyr Lewis and impromptu saviour in the mist!" He smiled at her, "Had you kept on in this direction you would have come to the village eventually, but not to worry, I've just come not far from the House and would be pleased to escort you there myself, Miss. . . ?"

She took his gloved hand and gave it a small shake.

"Watson. Thank you! But it isn't necessary to escort me, Sir, as kind as your offer is," she leant forward and gave Hefina a pat. "We will be perfectly fine, I am sure."

Her embarrassment was as such that she wished to put as much distance as she could between herself and the stranger and as she eased the mare round on the track, the young doctor did the same.

"No, I insist! How would I explain myself if you ended up in a bog, Miss Watson?"

"There are *Bogs*?" Beth reiterated with some alarm and then seeing his sidelong smile realised he was teasing her.

She gave a small laugh.

"I'm sorry to put you to all this trouble. I'm sure you have more important things to do."

"Perhaps," he said easily, "but it's not often you meet a fair-haired beauty on the moor. You gave me quite a start, Miss Watson; for a moment I thought my eyes were playing tricks and that it was *Branwen* herself coming through the mist!"

He was flirting with her. Need she be worried? She gave him a level look and saw only warm appreciation in the brown eyes, and she faced forwards again aware that she was blushing.

"So you are from the Galinas House, visiting, might I dare ask?"

There was an awkward pause before Beth found her voice.

"No, Sir, I am employed by the family."

"Ah. . ." said the young man thoughtfully, "then may I venture even further and ask how you are finding it?"

Beth found herself beginning to bristle. The man asked far too many questions.

"Well enough!" she said shortly and gave Hefina a squeeze. The mare picked up the pace and soon they had drawn away.

"Miss Watson! Have a care, please, my apologies if I've offended you!"

She could hear his voice but her attention was taken by a glow of lights that was coming their way and the rattling wheels of a trap. And then as she heard a familiar voice call out her she responded vigorously, loud in her relief!

Tegid! The kindly old man and head stableman had come out to look for her! And with him his grandson, Owen, and a stable hand mounted on a rangy grey.

"*Iesu Grist*, Miss Watson, are you alright?" he said as they pulled to a halt and she knew that she must look a sight.

'Yes, yes...I...'

Beth was assailed by all manner of emotions in that moment; but chief among them was acute embarrassment and as she stumbled over her words so keen was she to make her apologies, her companion caught up at that moment and all eyes widened as they took him in.

Tegid looked with muted concern from one to the other and Beth's heart sank even further as she realised how it might look.

"Why, Dr Lewis!" he said in surprise.

"None other and none too soon!" said the young man with a jovial air, and Beth spun round and looked at him aghast. *Dr Lewis*

"Miss Watson here was all set for the village when I came upon her in the mist, and a good job I did too!"

Beth looked at the old man appealingly, "I am so, *so* sorry! I was incredibly foolish. I should've listened and I can promise you it will never happen again. . ."

"Not to worry, Miss, you're not the first one to be caught out by the mists and you certainly won't be the last," said Tegid mildly. He sensed her distress and was touched by it. "You are safe and you are well, and that is the most important thing."

He looked to the young doctor.

"Our thanks, Sir,"

"My pleasure." he turned to Beth and tipped his hat. "Truly...Hwyl!"

Then with a smart move he wheeled his horse around and trotted off into the mist.

As the sound of the hoof beats slowly receded, Beth turned back to Tegid.

"I suppose I'll be in trouble now for having caused everyone such trouble. I really cannot apologise enough."

Tegid waved a hand.

"No harm done, just a fright for you, no doubt. Jake! Help Miss Watson down and Owen, you hop up on Hefina! Come along, Miss, let's get you on board and we'll soon have you back in the house!"

As soon as Beth was safely ensconced next to Tegid she did her best to rearrange her hair in to some kind of order and then in a low voice said,

"It was not as it looked, I promise you. The doctor found me, and well... You do believe me, don't you?"

"Have no fear, Miss. I have known Master Lewis since he was a boy and a gentleman he is, through and through. We will keep this quiet and say we came across only you on the moors. I know you'll be worrying what the mistress might say, but have no fear, my boy and Jake will say nothing."

"But what of the doctor? He knows the family! Will he say anything?"

The old man favoured her with an enigmatic smile.

"Don't flap so, Miss. He is an enlightened and discreet young man who has just come to the end of his apprenticeship with Dr Morgan, who is physician proper to the family. You have nothing to worry about there. He is a canny lad and very much his own man, I can assure you."

"What do you mean by that?" Beth asked.

The old man favoured her with one of his smiles.

"Just that, Miss Watson, just that..."

Chapter 6

The head stableman was as good as his word, and Beth's brief foray off the beaten track of the moors elicited no more than several tuts and a few raised eyebrows. She told Nanny Gwyn, of course, and of her encounter with the young doctor. She was apprehensive that he might say something during a house visit, but Nanny soothed her fears and when he did make the fortnightly call with Dr. Morgan, he did no more than apply himself in asking after the child before examining her with a gravity that belied his light manner on the moors.

"He is a nice young man and a very good doctor," said Nanny Gwyn, "he is especially interested in our Eleri and has more patience; but then he is more of the modern age perhaps and less inclined to the old ways."

Beth knew she was referring to Dr Morgan who had something of a no-nonsense air about him and little empathy, if any, with the child, and she had seen how Eleri had shrunk before him in a way she had not with Dr Lewis.

"The plan, of course, is that he will take over the practice completely once Dr Morgan retires, and for some of us," Nanny had added in an undertone, "the day cannot come soon enough!"

Beth understood for it was crucial that Eleri's fragile state be dealt with only within the realms of ultimate kindness and unlike his protégé, Dr Morgan had demonstrated little of that.

When the formal introductions had been made between Beth and the two physicians, Dr Lewis was courteously polite and betrayed by not so much of a flicker that they had met before, although his eyes did seem to linger momentarily on her neatly coiffered hair.

But what was certain, however, was that both doctors were evidently pleased at the improved colour in Eleri's cheeks and the discovery that she had gained a little weight.

"Why Nanny, you must be keeping Cook busy in the kitchen, or else she has come up with a magical new dish!" remarked Dr Morgan, "for the girl will soon be as fat as a little pig! Why, this is progress indeed!"

As Beth stared at him stupefied at his choice of words and then felt ridiculously grateful as Dr Lewis swiftly bent down to Eleri and gave her face a soft tickle, saying, "*Na, more like a soft little lamb, and there are few things as sweet as a lamb, eh, ychydig un?*"

"No, not Cook, Dr Morgan," said Nanny, "all credit must go to Miss Watson, I'll have you know! She works ceaselessly with our charge and takes her outside frequently, weather permitting. I am sure all of that fresh air must be beneficial for I was never able to take her so often and so it is Miss Watson you must thank!"

Both doctors turned to look at Beth and she blushed under their scrutiny as Dr Morgan regarded her with grudging admiration, the younger one with a sudden mischievous look in his eye.

"Why, then it is most certainly to your stirling efforts that we must commend you, Miss Watson!" he said brightly, "for you obviously have considerable talent in the accruement of lost souls!"

Beth searched his face for mockery; but there was none, just a hint of humour and genuine appreciation in the light brown eyes. She looked away, suddenly aware that the young doctor was considerably attractive and gave a small shrug.

"It is nothing more than simple kindness, Sir, and besides, Nanny Gwyn has much experience to impart and has been my guidance throughout so I cannot claim full credit."

"You are too modest, Miss Watson," Dr Lewis went on, "I also hear you've proposed a trip to greet an equine newcomer to the stables this afternoon. Sounds like an excellent idea; what do you think, Dr Morgan?"

The older doctor gave a small grunt before replying.

"Anything that can shake her out of her *Malaise* cannot be discounted. But I would not expect too much, Miss Watson, we have laboured for a year or more under all manner of treatments, but. . . " he closed his bag with a snap. "if you think it will help in some way, then by all means, carry on."

Beth bowed her head and then bending down she attended to Eleri as Nanny showed the physicians to the door.

The child had curled in on herself; the visits from the physicians had obviously disturbed her in some way, and although Dr Morgan had been proficient, his bedside manner left much to be desired and she was all the more grateful for the sensitivity of Dr Lewis.

Looking down into the wan little face her heart filled again with such tenderness she thought it would break.

"Eleri. . . " Her voice caught and she took a moment to compose herself, "we will help you and bring you out of this dark place yet." She squeezed the small fingers gently, "but in the meantime, can you trust me just a little bit more and allow me to take you beyond the gardens? I hear that this baby foal has the longest legs that you ever will see and that it has such a sweet disposition, it would be shame not to go and say hello. . ."

Beth gazed down at the lowered lids and there was just the slightest twitch and she felt elated. Having become so finely attuned to the merest hint of response that the child chose to convey, it was with confidence that she took this as a sign of concurrence, and as soon as luncheon was over she led her charge down through the gardens and to the gate that came out near the stables.

As soon as Tegid saw them he hurried across the yard his face wreathed in smiles and then bending down to Eleri he said, "And so at last we meet. . . and I am truly honoured, little miss, *ydy wir!* My name is Tegid and you are *most* welcome!"

Eleri turned shyly away into Beth's skirts and then peeped out at the old man before retreating once more and Tegid chuckled softly.

"Why, you are as skittish as my foal but she is as keen to meet you as you are to meet her, let me tell you!" And as his words drew another covert peep he lowered his voice further as though to share a secret. "And how do I know this?"

His manner was having the desired effect as he was rewarded with another peep, longer this time, and Beth marvelled at the evident charisma of this old horseman.

"Well, this is because horses have a secret language, see. A secret way of talking all of their own and, if you love them enough, care for them enough, and *listen* enough, sometimes you'll hear them, *and.* . . . if you're lucky enough; they will also speak to *you*!"

He had her attention now. Dark eyes held him fast, interest had somehow penetrated into the deep depths of indifference and seeing this the old man nodded knowingly.

"So when I told her you were coming today, she nudged my hand and said, tell her not to be afraid for I, too, have come into a strange new world where everyone is so much bigger than me. Oh yes, she was concerned, indeed she is *so* keen to make your acquaintance I dare not dally any longer, for she's a spritely little thing and wants *so much* to meet you, *cariad*! Shall we?"

He reached out a brown leathery hand and to Beth's amazement Eleri took it.

As Tegid straightened up the child now safely gathered between them, Beth gazed at him incredulously as without further ado he led the way to a small barn where they were greeted by the warm sweet smell of hay and an excited high-pitched whinny.

"See, *cariad*. She knows you are here before she has even seen you!" exclaimed Teg, and as they went into the dim interior they saw that a section had been fenced off and within its confines pranced a little filly roan. In the far corner her dam stood calmly grazing.

At the sight of the foal Beth felt Eleri stiffen with what she hoped was pleasure and then both she and Tegid released a hand each as the child edged forward and stood at the lower part of the enclosure.

The filly snorted and gambolled towards her before coming to a sudden halt. Child and foal regarded each other solemnly for some moments, and then with dainty precision the filly stepped forward and gave a small snort before she stretched out her muzzle, nostrils quivering, large eyes filled with interest.

Beth and the old stable-man watched with breathless anticipation as gradually, tentatively, and with agonising slowness, Eleri's hand appeared and reached out, and the foal stepped closer still and snuffled at the outstretched fingers before giving a gentle snort. It was a defining moment as this poor little girl finally made a connection at her own initiative and as though in recognition of this the foal became docile and stood quietly as Eleri stroked the soft nose.

Tegid looked at Beth and was surprised to see tears in her eyes; he touched her arm and indicated they move away so as to allow the child the magic of this encounter to herself. Beth followed the old man and they stood in the doorway as dust motes danced around them.

"Thank you," Beth murmured and pulled out a handkerchief and dabbed at her eyes, "I'm sorry, but I couldn't help myself."

"Sssshhh. . ." soothed the old man, "you have no need to explain, Miss, besides, they are happy tears, are they not?"

"They are indeed. . . my only hope was that the sight of the foal might interest or distract her. I would never have dreamed she should engage so quickly and *like this*! I cannot wait to tell Nanny Gwyn!"

As more tears fell Tegid patted her shoulder for he understood the strain she'd been under, as he did anyone subjected to the atmosphere of that house. Many a time had he lain in his pallet and been glad for his humble surroundings and the peace that came with it, except on those nights, of course. . .

"Just to see her reaching out gives such encouragement, such *hope*! There, now I've really made myself look *twp* blubbering like a silly fool!"

Beth looked at Tegid with a watery smile and he lifted his shoulders.

"I've had worse to deal with on this yard, let me tell you, Miss, and tears have been the least of them! Come, let us sit down here on this bench just here and enjoy the sun. The child is fine within and she knows we are close by," he gave Beth a warm look, "It was a fine idea to bring her here. Indeed I would even go as far as to say that you are the first nurse who had really bothered to make a difference; except for Nan, of course, but then she is at that time of life when all she should be concerning herself with are long afternoon naps and warming toes by an open fire." He gave a sudden chuckle, "Not unlike myself, but it's hard to throw off the harness when that's all you've ever known all your life."

"You were born here, Nanny tells me." said Beth tucking her kerchief back into her sleeve.

"Aye, as was my father and his father before him. We have been employed by the family for generations. My forefathers have always loved working with horses. They are, without doubt, one of the noblest creatures God put on this earth, and it is to my great fortune that the master keeps a good stable."

Beth regarded him solemnly.

"You are a very kind man," she said, "and if you are as good with horses as you are with troubled children, then it is of great fortune that the Master has *you!*"

Tegid grinned and shook his head.

"You are quite a character, I have to say and a much needed breath of fresh air; do you know that, Miss? And if we are going to go down the path of giving compliments, then the House also has much to thank *you* for!"

She knew what he meant by 'the house', of course. It was an idiom for the undercurrent of divided loyalties and hostility that ran through it and they exchanged a smile of mutual understanding.

"You look a little tired, Miss, if you don't mind my saying," Tegid said quietly, "not taking on too much, are you?

Beth dropped her head momentarily and then leaned forward and looked around the door to check on her charge. Eleri and the foal remained enraptured in each other like two long lost friends engaged in a silent but deeply profound communication, then turning back to the old man she went to speak and then paused suddenly unsure..

"It's alright, Miss, whatever it is, but if you feel you can't trust me, I'll. . ."

"Oh no, it isn't *that*!" said Beth hastily, "Strange as it sounds after so short an acquaintance, I feel as though I could trust you with my life! It's just that. . . well. . . I don't want you to think me frivolous, and it is definitely not my duties with the child that is disturbing me," she gave him an earnest look, "It's. . . it's something else."

"In the house. . ."

"Yes."

Somewhere across the yard a bucket was dropped followed by a curse, and in the distance a flock of starlings made their way noisily across the sky as the old man regarded Beth levelly.

"Go on "

"There have been things happening. . . random things, like my possessions being moved around as though to perplex me, I can make no sense of it. . ." she drew a deep breath and gestured in bewilderment "One morning I woke to find my hairbrush next to me on my pillow, and recently

I came to in the middle of the night and could've sworn there was a figure stood at the end of the bed watching me but I could have been mistaken, for when my eyes adjusted to the darkness there was no one there." She looked suddenly uncomfortable and lowered her voice.

"At first I thought it might be one of the servants playing tricks and so I have taken to leaving small objects behind the door each time I leave the room; things like hairpins or a small ball of cotton. I have also put things in place before retiring for the night, but despite all of my efforts, these measures have only served to increase the mystery as they continue to happen!" She paused and looked out across the yard a slight frown dimpling the smooth brow.

"Why, only this morning I found my riding boots neatly sat together in front of the door and with such precision, I confess I am at a complete loss as how they came to be there!"

The young woman turned her troubled gaze back to Tegid who nodded slowly his face set,

"Do they scare you, Miss...these strange happenings?."

"Sometimes," she said carefully, "although if I am honest, I am as intrigued by them as I am perturbed, for what is the reasoning behind it? Why would anyone want to try and frighten me like this?"

"To draw attention to themselves, perhaps..?"

Beth looked into the grizzled old face questioningly.

Tegid looked away his gaze settling on the stable clock above the arched entry to the yard.

Do you believe in ghosts, Miss?"

Beth was immediately thrown by the question and for some moments did not know what to say, "Well. . . why. . . I don't know, it is not something I've really thought about before, but. . ."

She broke off abruptly and studied him keenly, and then reaching out a hand she touched his sleeve saying, "*Do you*?"

But before he could answer they both heard a small noise and turned to see Eleri stood quietly in the doorway.

Rising swiftly Beth went to her and bent down so that she could see into her face.

"Is all well, Eleri? Are you alright?"

As usual there was no response and Beth wondered how long she'd been stood there and even more concerning was how much of the conversation she had heard!. Tegid stepped past her and into the barn and found the foal back suckling with its mother its tiny tail swishing furiously.

"All seems well; the little one has gone back to her mam to feed so I can only guess that your conversation must have given her an appetite, *cariad bach*!"

His tone was light but his expression was slightly worried as his eyes met those of Beth's for the last thing he wanted was to scare a small child with ghost stories.

"We'll speak again soon," he said meaningfully and Beth nodded.

"Why, all of this talk of appetite has given me a thirst for a nice cool glass of lemonade! And perhaps some of Nanny's special biscuits, if we're lucky! What say you, Eleri? Shall we go and see what we can rustle up!"

She straightened and took the child's hand.

"Thank you. . . Tegid,"

It was the first time she had addressed him by his Christian name, but it felt right and he looked pleased at this new level in their relationship.

"You have been most kind but we will not keep you any longer."

"It has been my pleasure, Miss; it's not often we see two pretty ladies in the stables at one time, so thank you for making friends with my foal and for brightening my day." He addressed the last part to Eleri who turned away shyly, but there was a pink hue in the cheeks that denoted pleasure and once again Beth marvelled at his ability to elicit a response.

"Here," he said, "let me walk you back over to the gate," but before any of them could move there was a cacophony of hooves and laughter as four riders clattered into the yard where they came to a halt at the sight of the trio.

Beth felt the child stiffen immediately and drew her in close. Even the old man's face seemed to darken as he called out for the grooms.

It was the children of the house and Beth's first proper sight of them since she'd arrived. Miss Meacham was with them looking regal in a finely-cut riding habit of pale lavender, but the quality of her attire did nothing to lift her complexion or the spite in her face, but Beth's eyes were on the children and her heart fell at what she saw.

Chapter 7

The older girl was the first to draw her attention as she sat her horse with a haughty air, a coldness emanating from the green eyes so like her mothers. Her hair was a dark auburn and her figure tall and lithe. She regarded Beth and the child with barely concealed contempt before turning away to bark instructions at a groom.

The boy in contrast was thickset and fair with a sulky set to the mouth. A flurry of prepubescent spots added colour to the already flushed cheeks that puffed disgust at finding them there.

Beth then looked to the youngest child who had already dismounted and was like a smaller version of her sister; only her hair was a more vibrant red and her eyes filled with nothing other than a vivid curiosity.

Despite Miss Meacham's obvious attempts to turn her attention elsewhere, the young girl continued to cast covert glances towards Beth and her charge and Beth sensed that she would have come over and spoken if she could.

"Clara, you did splendidly!" Miss Meacham enthused, "Tegid, can you believe that this child jumped Hector's fence today; and without not so much of a moment's hesitation!"

As the old man turned to congratulate the youngest girl, the boy, who remained in the saddle addressed his older sister in ringing tones not yet broken by impending manhood.

"I declare there is an odd stench in the yard, Lavinia, can you not smell it?"

He stared openly with unbridled spite towards Eleri and Beth's heart skipped a beat. She had not anticipated such direct animosity and pulling the child to the other side of her so as to shield her, she began to make her way around the medley of mounts and people towards the gate that led to the walled gardens.

"Yes, I believe there is. But it appears to be leaving now..." drawled the older girl, "I must have a word with mama about the state of this yard, there is obviously some kind of vermin infestation. What say you, Miss Meacham?"

The governess made some reply but Beth didn't hear her as she hastened in through the gate her cheeks burning with angered humiliation. So rude and so blatant! *How dare they!*

She hurried them both up the backstairs and straight to Nanny's rooms.

The old lady was sewing as she bid them enter and rose with concern at the look on Beth's face.

"Why, cariad, what is it?"

Beth realised that she was shaking, and taking a grip on herself made sure she took a deep breath before answering.

"We have just been insulted! Openly! Brazenly, and in front of the stable servants! Oh Nanny Gwyn, I could scarce believe my *ears! And in front of Eleri!*" She lowered her voice at the mentioning of the name and hugged the child to her.

"What? Who...?" said Nanny bewildered.

"The children! Or rather the boy and the eldest girl, they were insolent, and cruelly so! We met them in the stables. Just a minute or so earlier and we would have been away..."

Nanny shook her head sadly, "Oh Miss, what can I say, other than they are far beyond my influence and have been for some time now. Oh how I wish it were not like this, it is most unpleasant! Here, sit down, both of you and I will ring for some refreshment..." But before she could pull the bell cord there was a tap at the door.

It was Gwen and with a troubled look on the usually cheery features. Her hazel eyes found those of Beth's.

"The Mistress would see you, Miss."

"The Mistress?" echoed Nanny Gwyn.

"Yes, Mrs Gwyn, she said that Miss was to come immediately." The maid cleared her throat nervously and glanced apologetically at Beth as though in woe at being the messenger.

"Very well," said Nanny Gwyn briskly, "Gwen, take the child to the nursery and ring for some milk and biscuits, this should not take long."

Gwen's mouth dropped open as both she and Beth stared at the old lady in surprise.

"I think I know what this will be about and I am not willing to let Miss Watson face it alone. Now jump to it, Gwen, what are you are waiting for?"

As Gwen hustled Eleri out of the room Beth gathered herself and turning to Nanny Gwyn she laid a hand on her arm.

"Please, I am most grateful, but you do not have to do this."

There was a fierce light in Nanny Gwyn's eyes that Beth hadn't seen before and she found this unexpected change in her demeanour quite startling.

"No, Miss, I believe I do! Now pass me my shawl, will you, and let us go see what this is all about."

Beth was filled with apprehension as they made their way to the East wing of the house and certain confrontation but Nanny unerringly led the way, her plump little chin held high with a firm air of resolve.

As they came to the mistress's door the old lady reached out and gave Beth's hand a small squeeze before administering a polite knock.

"Come!" The response was immediate and as both women stepped into the shady confines of the salon it was to find the Mistress sat at her bureau with the governess, still in her riding habit stood to the side. Their eyes widened as Beth and Nanny Gwyn came in together, and laying down her quilled pen the mistress turned towards them from her seat as two blots of red appeared on the pale cheeks.

"What is this? I sent for Miss Watson not you Nanny Gwyn. Why are you here?"

The tone was clipped and bristled with displeasure but the old nurse was not fazed and replied stoically.

"I am concerned that Miss Watson may have inadvertently caused some offence and I wish only to support her, ma'am, and provide her with a defence, if needed."

Miss Meacham emitted a small sound from her throat as the mistress raised her eyebrows rendered speechless for some moments. The green eyes narrowed.

"Is that so? Why you surpass yourself, Nanny, I had no idea you and Miss Watson were so. . . *attached!* And you, do you feel the need for some *defence*, Miss Watson? Loitering around the stables like some serving wench when you should be attending to your duties certainly sounds indefensible to *me!* What have you got to say for yourself?"

"Why, it was nothing more than a distraction for the child, and I thought only to. . ."

"What? Speak up, girl, I can barely hear you!"

"She says. . ." began Nanny and the mistress cut across her like a knife.

"I am addressing the nurse, Nanny Gwyn, and would thank you to hold your peace! The girl has a tongue, has she not? Let her use it. Well?"

Beth drew a deep breath and raised her voice slightly. The tension in the room was palpable as she was caught between the age-old battle between the favoured retainer and mistress of the house.

"I meant no harm, ma'am, I thought only to provide some means of stimulation, by showing Emily the new foal, and as Tegid said it would. . ."

"Tegid!" broke in the mistress sharply, "Since when has Tegid assumed authority in this house?" She glanced back at the governess with a look of incredulity and then returning her attention to Beth shook her head in disbelief.

"Ma'am, if I may speak?" interjected Nanny.

The mistress cast an irritable look in her direction and gave a long-suffering sigh.

"Yes, what is it, Nanny."

"Only that both Dr. Morgan and Dr. Lewis expressed great pleasure at the idea and thought it would be beneficial to the child. It is just a misfortune of timing that Miss Meacham and the children happened to come upon them as they were about to return to the house."

This disclosure had the desired effect as the mistress frowned and looking back again to Miss Meacham she said, "The doctor's gave their permission; you did not say?"

"I. . . I did not know. . ." stuttered the governess and the sharp features flushed with colour as she dropped her eyes to the floor.

"Precisely," said Nanny Gwyn quietly, "you did not know."

In the awkward silence that followed Beth watched as the mistress, having been thrust into an embarrassing situation now sought to remove herself from it with some modicum of dignity.

"I now see that I have been clearly misinformed," she intoned stiffly, "but the fact remains I do not want my children to be in sight, or anywhere within the vicinity of that brat. Therefore, Miss Watson, in future you will ensure that any further visits to the stables do not coincide with my children's activities, and Nanny Gwyn, I charge you with the task that it does not happen again!"

The old nurse bowed her head and lowered her eyes so that the mistress would not see the triumph in them, and as Beth went to speak the mistress held up a hand.

"There is nothing further to say on the matter. I bid you both leave now." And no sooner were the two women outside the door than they heard angry tones as the mistress berated Miss Meacham.

Moving swiftly away down the corridor Beth still couldn't quite believe how Nanny had handled the interview and she glanced at the old lady admiringly. She waited until they were back in the relative safety of Nanny's room before she dared to give voice.

"Oh, Nanny, I thought that was going to be the end of me and my time here. How can I ever thank you!"

The old woman grasped her hands and gave them a small shake.

"By remaining vigilant, and at all times! Know that Miss Meacham has seen off many a servant including your predecessors but she certainly seems to have taken a particular dislike to you. *Arglwydd,* but she must have gone running to the mistress no sooner than you'd left the stables!"

Nanny shook her head in disgust and released Beth's hands as she regarded her steadily.

"I cannot warn you enough, and now that she has been humiliated by her folly she will seek only to ensure your downfall and removal from the house."

"What can make a person so vindictive, Nanny?" said Beth sadly, "she has security in her position and the confidence of those who employ her. I fail to understand her and the reasons for her malice. Why is she so bitter?"

Nanny Gwyn went to her comfy armchair and sat down, the kindly face suddenly overcome by a weary look.

"Envy, unhappiness, desire for a different life, perhaps. But there is reward in currying favour with the mistress for she is not without generosity to those she deems loyal." The old lady turned her gaze on to Beth.

"You saw the fine riding habit she was wearing; just one of the many gifts a governess can only usually dream of. . . we may have won this battle, Miss Watson, but we are far from winning the war. In future we shall be more careful, but in the meantime, best you go fetch Eleri and I will make us some much-needed tea. Perhaps you would also be so good as to bring the *Mabinogion* and read to us awhile? I am overcome by the need to immerse myself in worlds far away from the one in which we find ourselves."

"Nanny, after that display I would read you the whole book *and* in one sitting!" Beth cried before hurrying up to the nursery.

Later as they drowsed before the fire and with Eleri fast asleep in her arms, Beth ventured to share the strange conversation she had had with Tegid earlier that day.

"You don't think me silly or prey to my imagination, do you, Nanny?" she asked careful to keep her voice low.

There was a long pause before the old lady made a reply.

"There is a story associated with this house but I'm vague on the details, such is the price of getting old." Nanny Gwyn gave a sweet smile and turned back to the fire. "But then it is a very old house so I suppose there may be a ghost or two."

"So it is possible then? That what is going on in my room could be something. . . not of this world?" Just hearing herself saying the words Beth felt a slight shiver go through her and Nanny Gwyn shrugged.

"Who knows. . . we live in a land that is full of myth and legend. The *Mabinogion* is proof of that. But whatever it is I don't get the feeling of it meaning any harm. Maybe, as Tegid says, it is merely trying to attract your attention."

Beth studied the old lady for some moments.

"You do not seem unsettled by the prospect at all, Nanny. Why you are made of much sterner stuff than I could ever hope to be!"

"That is because it is the living who gives me greater cause for concern than any shade from the past. And if there are any restless ghosts in this house, then they have certainly not made themselves known to me. Perhaps you should speak with Tegid again, *cariad,* he has a great knowledge of this house and its history, and in the meantime try not to worry; I'm sure that if whatever it is means you any harm it would have done so by now."

Despite the old lady's attempt to impart comfort Beth retired that night her thoughts so full she doubted she would sleep. But as exhaustion took over the young woman drifted off to the tones of a speckled thrush as it trilled its last song into the darkening night, and a hush descended over the rest of the house as owls swooped over the moors without and not so much stirred as a mouse when suddenly there was a noise and Beth woke up immediately.

It came from the door.

It was the thud of a book falling over that she had lain against it earlier, and as she sat upright eyes straining the darkness, all but forgetting to how to breathe, time became suspended as she watched with a kind of fascinated horror as the door slowly began to open.

The moon came out from behind the clouds at that moment and Beth had never been so glad she slept with the drapes open, for the silvery light that now poured into her room showed her the small figure of Eleri

She expelled the breath she'd been holding her heart beating fast, and watched as the child closed the door behind her and simply stood as though awaiting further invitation. There followed an uncertain silence as Beth wondered if her charge was even awake, but then she saw the glisten of tears as the moon illuminated the sad little face and without hesitation she drew back the bedclothes back and waited.

With a slow step Eleri came forward and then climbed into the bed as Beth wordlessly gathered her into her arms and pulled the blankets around her; and as the child silently wept, the young woman gentled her with a lullaby and knew in her heart that whatever happened, she would take on all the mean mistresses and cruel governesses of the world if it meant protecting her charge, and so absorbed was she in the task at hand that she failed to see the other small figure that watched closely from the darkness.

Chapter 8

Thankfully it was Gwen who came with Beth's hot water the next morning, and her face showed almost comedic surprise when she saw Eleri peeping out from the pillows.

"What's this?" she said and emitted a small crow of delight, "T'would seem you have a cuckoo in your bed, Miss, and no mistake!"

Beth smiled and then said, "Yes, but it's a secret cuckoo, Gwen. No one must know where she nests in the night."

She gave the maid an earnest look. "You won't say anything, will you? I'll tell Nanny, of course, but I can't see the harm. . ."

"Don't know what you're talking about, Miss!" said the maid briskly, "but I'd best go and get your breakfast trays before the young miss wakes up next door and finds that she's hungry!" She followed up this announcement with a wink before disappearing back out of the door, and Beth hugged the small child to her happily.

"Good old Gwen! Come on, then, *bach*, we'd both best get up and dressed before anyone else comes looking!"

As Beth took care of her ablutions and chose her dress for the day, Eleri sat in the window seat looking out across the moors. Just the fact she had her gaze on anything but the floor was miraculous in itself, not to mention her night time visit to Beth driven by her need to be comforted. Both were huge steps forward and Beth couldn't wait to tell Nanny.

"Why, we must celebrate!" she cried once she'd heard the news, "and as it's such a beautiful day why not a picnic on the moors!"

The old woman bent down to Eleri beaming and chucked her under the chin.

"And what do you say to that, *cariad?* A little trip, yes?"

The dark eyes regarded her solemnly but there was a hint of something lighter in their depths.

"Miss Watson, if you would be so kind as to go down to the kitchens and arrange a basket with Cook, I will ring for a message to be sent to Teg so he can get the trap ready!"

She clapped her hands together in glee her cheeks glowing with excitement and Beth couldn't help but be swept along by her enthusiasm as she hurried down to the backstairs to the hustle and bustle of the house kitchens.

Her appearance was greeted with pleasure, even the housekeeper; Mrs Davis favoured her with a rare smile as she passed through. Word had abounded of her efforts and how well she was doing with the child, and the servants, ever empathetic to the underdog had taken Eleri and her plight to their hearts and her progress was often the topic of conversation around the dinner table.

"A picnic, you say? That will make a nice change, Miss." said Cook smilingly as she rolled out pastry. "Leave it with me, I'll have it ready for you in no time. Lizzy!" she called out, "Go and fetch the hamper and a clean table cloth! And Carys, six bottles of lemonade from the cooler, please!"

As the kitchen maids scurried about to do her bidding Cook lowered her voice and said, "It's wonderful what you're doing with the child, Miss. Poor little mite has had such a time of it and it breaks our hearts to see her treated so. Hope you will stay, Miss, really. . .we all do."

Beth, aware of the dangers of gossiping with servants, no matter how kindly their intent, flashed her a grateful smile.

"Only if you promise to put in some of your lovely Welsh cakes, Mrs Giles, because you know how much I love those and a picnic would not be the same without them!"

Cook beamed as Beth made a tactical withdrawal from the kitchen and when she returned to the nursery it was to find Nanny and Eleri sat looking at a picture book as they waited for her.

"You might want to take a shawl, Miss, it can get quite breezy on the moors." said Nanny getting up, "and we have ours, Eleri, have we not?"

Eleri's eyes remained on the book before her but there was a slight hunch in the shoulders that Beth read as suppressed excitement and her heart sang as she went to her room for her shawl before stopping in astonishment.

There draped across the end of her bed was her dark blue shawl as though waiting for her and Beth stood for some moments frozen in shock.

How? What?

She spun round, her eyes searching and then let out a nervous little laugh for the sight of her shawl having somehow removed itself from her trunk to the bed was as inexplicable as it was unsettling and she shook her head in bewilderment.

"Is everything alright? Are you ready, Miss?" Nanny's voice came floating down the hall, and drawing herself together Beth gave a wry smile before sweeping up the shawl and closing the door quietly behind her. She resolved to revisit the conversation she had begun with Tegid as soon as possible. The whole business was becoming more than bizarre, for it was almost as though the shawl had been out for her especially and she knew with certainty that Nanny would not enter her room uninvited.

"Coming!" she called and put the incident to the back of her mind for later.

As they made their way down the stairs and into the gloomy great hall, the door to the library opened and Miss Meacham stepped out carrying several books and she paused at the sight of them the pale face pinched with disapproval.

"Day out?" she ventured coldly.

"Just a picnic, Miss Meacham, along with pleasant company!" replied Nanny archly and the governess flushed.

"Does the mistress know?" she demanded.

"I doubt it," said Nanny as they made their way towards the door, "but then neither does the master and you can wager your soul he'll not have issue with it. Now if you'll excuse us, Miss Meacham, we don't want to waste a minute more of this beautiful day, so please, don't let us keep you from your duties!"

Beth bit back the laughter that bubbled in her throat as she glanced back to see Miss Meacham gaping in their wake like a floundered fish! Once again she was in awe of the little old woman and her feisty spirit as they came out into the sunshine just as Tegid brought the trap round and came to a smart halt.

There was light chatter as they bowled easily along one of the moorland paths blue skies stretching out as far as the eye could see. Beth sat up front with Tegid as Nanny cuddled Eleri in the back and despite the child maintaining her silence she looked about occasionally, brief glimpses taken from beneath the brim of her straw hat.

"It really is very lovely up here!" Beth observed and craned her head back to watch a large bird of prey hovering amidst the thermals.

"When it's like this, I have to agree, Miss, but it can also be dangerously deceptive and a cruel place."

Beth looked askance at the old man but he said nothing further, and as they topped a small rise there rose suddenly in the distance a dramatic array of rugged mountains wreathed in purple heather and crowned with a fine mist.

Beth drew breath.

"The Clwydian Mountains," said Nanny with a hint of wistfulness in her voice, "and home, for me once, just beyond the largest peak there."

"Why, it's beautiful, Nanny. Such grandeur! It makes the Brecon Beacons from where I come from look quite demure!" Turning back in her seat she addressed the old lady directly. "Perhaps we can visit another day; when we have more time? Would that be possible, do you think, Nanny?"

"I am amazed you think even to ask the question!" exclaimed Tegid, "Anything is possible with Nanny Gwyn!" and the two women laughed delightedly.

"I don't see why not, but for now let us be content with Gypsy Hollow for if I'm not mistaken that is where we're going, is it not, Tegid?"

"It is indeed." And with a cluck and a shake of the reins the old man guided the dark cob away from the mountains and towards a dell of trees from where came the sound of gurgling water.

"There's a lovely little stream here where you'll be able to dabble your feet. Maybe we'll even see some fish!" Nanny said to Eleri who was now beginning to take in her surroundings with more and more interest and in that moment Beth experienced the first flush of real happiness since coming to the house.

As Nanny took charge of laying out the blanket and the hamper, Tegid settled the horse and trap next to the water before pulling out his pipe and finding a grassy knoll to sit on and enjoy a smoke.

Beth explored the sun-dappled dell with Eleri pointing out birds and flowers as she did so.

"Look! There's a badger sett, although I'm sure they'll all be fast asleep now. And oh, how pretty is this, Eleri! Have you ever seen a butterfly this colour before?"

The child made no answer but her eyes were bright and her head turned each time in response to Beth's comments, and it dawned on the young woman that the key to releasing her charge from her silence was to remove her from the house. The hostility; the atmosphere; the constant underlying sense of resentment. Who wouldn't be affected beneath such a cloud! And the young woman vowed that she would do all she could to ensure her charge had the necessary freedom in order to thrive away from the house.

Nanny was calling so they made their way back and sat on the blanket an array of fruits and cheeses laid out before them. Teg ambled over still puffing on his pipe as Nanny scolded him good-heartedly.

"And you can put that smelly old thing away! If I want smoke around me when I'm eating I'll sit next to a chimney!" she cried handing out hunks of homemade bread and the old man rolled his eyes before tapping out the ashes and stepping them into the ground.

Beth selected some ham and a crumbly cheese for Eleri and began to peel an apple.

"This is a fine place for a picnic. Is it a favourite spot, then?" Beth enquired conversationally.

She then sliced the fruit and placed half on the child's plate.

"It is if you want shade and water for the horses," said Teg around a mouthful of bread. "Not what I'd call my favourite place, but Nan, here, is rather fond of it."

"That's because it has a sense of the romantic about it, and don't you dare say otherwise, Teg Ifans!"

As the old man snorted Beth looked questioningly at Nanny Gwyn who had a look of mischief in her eyes.

"Why, this is where the gypsies would come and set up camp when I was a girl! They'd have music and dancing and fires that would last into the night, and sometimes they'd come as far as the village selling their wares and glimpses of the future for a price. For a child with any sense of adventure, such visitors were always exciting, and yes, I confess, I found them fascinating and would have run away with them if I could!"

Beth spluttered into her lemonade as Nanny gave a giggle that was distinctly girlish and even Eleri raised her head to see what the fuss was all about.

"*Duw*, woman!" said Tegid shaking his head and Beth laughed out loud enjoying the banter between them. That they shared a particular bond, she had no doubt, and it was just so liberating to be able to relax away from prying eyes and the general gloom of the house and as a thought crossed her mind she suddenly leaned forward with excitement!

"Nanny! Tegid! I have just had the most *wonderful* idea! And!" she beamed down at her charge, "it involves you, Eleri!"

"Oh, and what's this, then?" said Nanny with interest as the child stopped chewing and listened intently.

"There is a smaller trap, is there not? The one you came in when you picked me up from the station, Tegid!" her eyes were shining as she looked at the old man and he thought he'd never seen a girl more naturally beautiful and full of life. He smiled at her fondly.

"Yes, Miss, and what of it?"

"Well, if you taught me how to drive it I could take Eleri out! Just imagine how beneficial that will be! No more being stuck in the house trying to avoid prying eyes! And you are enjoying this excursion, are you not, *cariad?*" As all eyes went to the small figure as she sat like a small doll her plate of food barely touched before her and they were rewarded by just the merest dip of the head. Beth clasped her hands together looking from Teg to Nanny and then back again.

"I don't see why not," offered Tegid smoothing his moustaches, "as long as Meg is between the shafts and it wouldn't take long to get the hang of the reins and suchlike," he gave Nanny a canny look, "although it might be worth running it past the Squire first, I'm thinking. . ."

"My thoughts exactly," said Nanny, "He is due back tomorrow. I will seek him out and ensure his approval." She leaned across giving Beth's arm a warm squeeze, "I think it is a marvellous idea and I'm sure the master will, too!"

They continued their picnic with animated chatter as some of the bolder birds flew down from the trees and pecked amongst the crumbs, and once everyone had eaten their fill and re-packed the hamper Beth asked Tegid if she could speak with him alone.

"If you don't mind staying with Eleri just for a few minutes, please, Nanny?" she added.

"Now why should I mind," replied Nanny with a chuckle, "when I've been waiting for the chance to put my toes in that nice, cool water! And you'll join me, won't you, Eleri *bach*? We will pretend we are like the gypsy-folk who came here and shall bare our legs to the sun!"

Beth smiled as Tegid shook his head in bemusement and taking his pipe from his pocket stood up and stretched as Eleri and the old nurse walked down to the stream.

"Shall we?" he said and led the way to a fallen stump that provided the perfect seat, and seeing the tobacco come out Beth waited respectfully until he'd filled and then lit his pipe, drawing on it with obvious pleasure.

"I think you know what it is I am going to ask you," Beth began, "and even now I can hardly believe that I am about to have this conversation! For my father frowned upon such things, you see, being a religious man he would regard anything like ghosts and spirits as being the work of the devil. My mother on the other hand. . ." and she paused looking out across the purple-tinged heath to the mountains beyond and gave a small shrug.

"She was of a different mind, although she knew better than to voice her thoughts when my father was around. But since he's been gone, we have shared many conversations on the subject, for in my grief I wanted, *needed* to know whether I would ever see him again!"

In her earnestness she looked very young and Tegid had to remind himself that for all she had the substance of a woman beyond her years she was still only nineteen and fresh to the world.

"My mother told me that such things do exist, and that not all of them were of the devil. She said that her *Nain* used to read the fire, that she would see things in the flames, glimpses of what might be. . . that it was a gift of sorts. . ." She broke off and regarded the old man apprehensively.

"You don't think I'm making this up, do you, Tegid?"

He removed the pipe from his mouth and a quiver of smoke slipped from between his lips.

"I can assure you that you need have no fear of that, Miss. Go on."

Casting him a grateful look Beth then returned her gaze to the moors as her voice took on a confidential tone with just a hint of some unexpressed emotion beneath it. Without seeming to do so Tegid watched her closely.

"Well, my mam also told me that she saw something of this gift in me. . . said I had the gift of *knowing,* and that I must not be afraid of it, for such gifts were not frowned upon in certain places and that our female line had always been blessed in this way. . ." She stole a glance at Teg and he nodded encouragingly.

"I've always dismissed it. My father was very strict about these things and well, any feelings or insights I may have had I always put down to coincidence. But I've discovered, especially since coming to the house that this *gift* is attracting something or *someone* to my room, and that as much as I'd prefer to remain in denial that such things exist. . ." suddenly she favoured the old man with a penetrating look. "You, however, have no such doubts and know exactly what's going on. . . *don't you, Tegid!"*

Chapter 9

The old stableman was taken aback despite himself, at her directness as much as anything else, and needing a moment to recover himself he foraged for more tobacco all the while held firm within the young woman's stare.

Finally he dropped his eyes as he replenished his pipe and gave a small smile.

"Why, Miss, you are more full of surprises than I would ever have imagined, although I sensed there was something different about you from the moment you stepped down from the train."

"Is that why you tried to warn me?" Beth asked in a quiet voice.

"Aye." replied the old man and striking a match he focused on the business of drawing the tobacco as Beth waited.

She had the feeling he was searching deep within himself for the right words. That they were about to embark on a conversation that was usually frowned upon, if not dismissed out of hand, did not escape her. And yet sat here amidst the wildness of the moors with a breeze soughing softly beneath a cloudless sky, it didn't seem peculiar at all, and for the first time in her life since her father had died, she felt a kinship with this man and it comforted her.

"You're right about the gift; as is your mam and her mam before her, for it has visited itself upon the male part of my forefathers, and so in answer to your question, Miss; yes, I do, I do know what is going on."

They gazed at each other in the unspoken forging of a bond as the final few links fell into place. Beth, with an almost reverent sense of relief, and the old man with much the same as a silence drew out between them broken only by the call of a red kite as it circled high above them.

"There is a ghost in the house. . . maybe there is more than one, but there is one that makes itself known; or perhaps I should say 'he'."

"He?" echoed Beth. "Is it a man?"

"No, *cariad,*" said Tegid gently, "it's a boy."

"A boy. . . " Beth breathed and looked out across the moors shaking her head in astonishment "I know not why, but I had believed it to be a *girl!"*

She turned back and looked searchingly into the face of the old man and he gazed back steadily.

"What does he want?"

"To be free."

A silence that thrummed with a thousand questions drew out between them as Beth knitted her brows more and more perplexed by the minute.

"Free? How so? I don't understand."

Tegid shifted on the log and took a long draw on the pipe as his eyes roamed the landscape.

"There is a tale; a legend some might say and dismiss it to be so. But I and my forefathers have full knowledge and know it to be true. I will not insult you, Miss, by asking for an assurance of your discretion, but I would respectfully ask that what I am about to reveal remains a secret between us and that you share it with nobody else; not even Nanny Gwyn."

Beth nodded. It surprised her greatly that Nanny would not be included in the confidence, but then he obviously had his reasons and for now she would have to respect that.

"You have my word."

"A long time ago, when you would still see troubles flare upon these Marches, Galinas House was lived in at the time by a man called Jacob Delfont. He was a cruel and violent man; much a man of his time and ruled his domain with a rod of iron, and like many men of power he hoarded wealth and drew prestige from it. He also had an eye for fine horses, and one day when the gypsies were passing over the moors, he saw amidst their motley herd the most magnificent stallion he had ever seen, and being the nature of the man he was, immediately coveted it for his own.

"He offered what he deemed a reasonable price, but the gypsies were loath to impart with their most precious possession, and so that night, as the travellers made camp in this very hollow, Delfont paid them an unexpected visit and took the stallion anyway. And as he and his men rode off laughing leaving mayhem in their wake, enraged, the head gypsy called out a curse upon him and the house!"

The old man cast a bemused glance at Beth as she listened spellbound.

"Despite the belief in such superstitions of the day, Delfont laughed it off, such was his arrogance, and to his stable he added this magnificent creature telling all who would listen that the gypsies had probably stolen it anyway!"

Tegid shook his head.

"But the beast was all but wild, ferocious if you dared to try and handle it, and so it was kept locked up and came out only to service the mares, for the master would not risk it escaping out to the moors and falling back into the hands of the travelling folk. . .but then one day someone did not lock the door properly and the stallion got out.

The yard was enclosed, as it still is today, and with the beast all but kicking up a storm as it careered around all hooves and teeth the grooms fled for cover as my forefather, as experienced as he was, struggled to get near it when suddenly into the yard comes Delfont's only son; a rather delicate boy, by all accounts, who having heard all the commotion had come to see what all the fuss was about. . ."

Once again the old man paused and then gave a wry chuckle.

"What, what is it?" asked Beth keen not to miss a single detail.

"Life, Miss, the fickleness of fate! That this child should be borne of such a man as Delfont and yet possess such qualities as to make him stand apart was quite extraordinary, for he was a meek boy, a gentle soul, without a nasty bone in his body. Some would say that he was a little *twp,"* The old man tapped his head.

"Was there a chance that he was not. . ." began Beth and the old man shook his head vigorously.

"I know what you were going to say, Miss, and the answer is no. The boy was his flesh and blood, alright. Apparently his wife was as securely contained in the house as the stallion was in its prison, and besides, he was his mother's boy and on that day he stepped out into the yard and the path of the raging beast, it was without a doubt those qualities that saved his life!"

Another pause and he stopped to draw deeply on his pipe as Beth had to resist the urge to grab his arm and shake it.

"Animals are canny creatures. They sense good in a person as they can sniff out evil intent, no matter well you are practised in the art of deceit, and this fine beast was no exception. And so picture the scene if you will; an angry and unbridled terror on four legs, so powerful, it could kill a man with one kick, and one small boy, puny for his age and helpless in the face of such fury that even my forefather, as seasoned as he was in handling all manner of wild horses was struck down with fear and could no sooner have moved from the spot than if Delfont had come at him with his whip!

There was a moment of silence as the beast took sight of the boy. No one dared draw breath and the very air was filled with dread as the beast gave off a terrible scream before it rushed at the boy and then astonished everyone by coming to a sudden halt before him!"

Tegid pulled at his moustaches, wonderment in his eyes before going on.

"I can almost see it now, this huge, powerful horse full of rage after months of being locked away, blowing and snorting like the devil himself, eyes rolling in their sockets and then slowing as they fixed on the boy who stood quietly and immovable before him. And then, almost too incredible to behold, the stallion lowered his great head and sniffed at the child who made some soothing sounds before reaching out and stroking the muzzle of this great beast, and then even more unbelievable still, the stallion became calm and allowed himself to be gentled by this mere slip of a boy. . . and they were stood thus when the master came on the scene his sword drawn at the ready before my forefather held him back!"

The old man gave a poignant smile.

"By all accounts he was highly regarded by the master, but then good horse-men, *natural* horse-men were hard to come by, and so he took no offence and heeded the warning, for to have gone in sword swinging would have placed the child in mortal danger and he was after all, his only son and heir. And so he stayed his hand and watched as this remarkable scene played out before them as the boy gentled the beast with little more than soft words and a hand that could've been ripped off in seconds."

"And then what happened?" urged Beth breathlessly.

"Well, in that instant the stallion all but claimed the boy, and the boy, the beast! And there began the most incredible friendship for the stallion was docile with him and the boy could do anything with him. Within days there was a saddle on his back and a bit in his mouth and a common sight as they rode the moors; this slip of a boy with a horse no one else could tame and his father, *his father!"* Teg chuckled, "Was all a-puff with pride that his milk-sop of a son had finally shown some steel and mastered the wildness of this beast, all but forgetting that it was not with steel by which he did so; just innocence and love with no desire to dominate."

"What an extraordinary little boy! He sounds...exceptional."

"Well, for his time and under the circumstances, yes, I suppose he was, but if you are hoping for a happy ending to this tale, Miss, I'm sorry but I am going to have to disappoint you."

"I had a feeling you were going to say that." Beth said heavily.

"Some months later the boy was up riding on the moors with a few retainers, when they came across the same band of gypsies who just happened to be passing through, and of course, they recognised their horse immediately!

There was a skirmish and the boy and the men were heavily outnumbered. As the gypsies mobbed them the boy fell and hit his head rendering him unconscious. Having taken back the stallion the gypsies fled the scene leaving the servants with nothing more than a few bruises but full of fear of what they'd tell the master; for they knew not at this point whether the boy was dead or alive. . ."

The old man paused and looked at her sadly.

"He may well have been the latter, for once they'd carried him back to the house and he regained consciousness it soon became apparent that he would never be the same again. He had no control over his bodily functions; he was weak, easily confused and became bed-bound. There was nothing the physicians could do, despite the raging of his father, for the injury to his head had caused such damage that there was little they could do other than tend to basic his needs and make him comfortable."

"Oh poor lamb!" breathed Beth.

"Yes, poor lamb indeed! But that isn't the end of it. Delfont, of course, had demanded of his men what exactly had taken place on the day of the attack, but rather than expose themselves to his fury and admit they'd been bested by a band of gypsies, they had decided on a story whereby the horse had taken fright and thrown the boy!"

Beth felt her eyes widen as Tegid shook his head slowly.

"Their version was not questioned and of course the boy was in no fit state to say otherwise. Everyone knew the stallion could be fiercely unpredictable and the false testimony of these men gave Delfont the opening he needed. His wrath was unassailable for he had, to all intents and purposes, lost his only son and so there was only thing a man of his nature would do, and so he set out and with only one purpose in mind."

The young woman clutched at his sleeve her eyes flooded with a sudden dread.

"Yes, I'm afraid so, Miss," he said gently, "and they found him, not two miles from the house, and running wild for the gypsies had not been able to hold him."

"Oh Teg," cried Beth and there were tears in her eyes, "this is going to be awful, I just know it!"

"Aye, you're not wrong there, Miss, but if you are to know the whole story then I must take you through to the end."

She nodded, her hands clasped tightly, her eyes tragic.

"Well, as I said, they came across the beast and the master let forth such a shout that the horse immediately gave flight; for as much as they can sense a kindly soul, well they know also when badness is before them, and so the stallion turned and took off across the moors with Delfont and his men hot in pursuit.

They ran him down, as you would any wild beast. They ran him to exhaustion until he could run no more, and then knowing still not to go too close, they caught him not with ropes but with *chains! With chains, for the love of God!* And then. . . and then. . ."

The old man's voice all but broke and he drew a deep breath. A flock of starlings screeched across the skies as though in sympathetic cacophony and Beth felt her heart begin to sink.

"They bound him to a tree and whipped at him mercilessly for they knew that such was the spirit of this magnificent beast that he would fight until his dying breath, and so he did as the chains bit deeper and they kept at him until he could fight no more and strangled himself to death. . ."

In the silence that followed it was as though the world itself was holding its breath as Beth stared at Tegid, deeply shocked.

"This story has been a legacy that has been handed down in my family from generation to generation, and no matter how many times I try to understand the actions of a grieving father, I will never, ever, until my dying day, know what could possess a man to such cruelty. When word reached the boy of what his father had done, even in his altered state he understood enough and was so beset by grief he lost what will he had to live and pined away unto death. Ah *Arglwydd*, so two lives lost for the reckless rage of one man!" Tegid's tone had become angry, "And, when the master learned of his son's death he departed from the house, the coward that he was never to return, leaving only one other person who knew the truth of what had happened to the boy on that fateful day."

"Your forefather. . ." murmured Beth and the old man nodded.

"Oh, and he knew, alright, for he had always had good relations with the gypsies that passed through the moor. Like us, they are horse-people; they would exchange equine-lore and poultices, gossip and news from the outside world, and it wasn't long before he was in full possession of the facts. But he held his peace, for what good would it have done? The boy was dead; no further acts of vengeance would bring him back."

The old man and his young companion sat in silence for some moments as the world slowly came back to life around them.

"It's him, isn't it?" said Beth eventually, "the ghost that comes to my room. . .it's the little boy."

Tegid pulled on his empty pipe now cold but still comforting and dipped his head. His eyes were faraway and there was a tear on his cheek.

"I would like to know his name, if he has one. . . does he, Tegid? Does this poor little spirit boy have a name?"

It was some moments before he made his reply.

"His name has been lost to history, I'm afraid, although there's doubtless some record of it somewhere, probably in the local church."

"And he is haunting me, but why?"

The old man turned to face her and Beth was struck by a sudden strange light in his eyes.

"Why, for the very same reason that the stallion haunts me, Miss! They are trapped in the fabric of their own tragedy. Bound together and yet kept apart by the very walls of hate and ignorance that put them there. They cannot rest and they have not done so for these past four hundred years, and it is my belief that it is your gift that has drawn the spirit-boy in, for he senses in you a way out, perhaps, a release."

"A release!" echoed Beth incredulously, "How. . . what. . . in what way?"

The old man regarded her and his eyes were sympathetic.

"You'll need to ask him that question, Miss, for God knows I wish I knew the answer. My family have been cursed by the sight of that poor wretched creature since it gasped its last breath, and every year, on the anniversary of this terrible deed, the shade of the stallion roams the moors screaming like a wild beast; doomed to run forever on a land where once it galloped free. You are the key, I believe, Miss, and it is my reckoning that this little boy knows it, too. I have heard it said that there are some spirits that see you but cannot speak, and there are others who can appear and engage as though they were still a part of this earth, and so, if there is chance of releasing these two spirits; should we not at least try to cross the breach?"

He waited as Beth looked off across the moors her face troubled.

"You ask much," she said gravely, "I have yet to accept this *gift* that has been thrust upon me, and now I am being asked to seek conversation with the shade of a boy who died in the house almost half a century ago." she shook her head.

"It is a strange and tragic tale that you have told me, and I do believe that whatever or *whomever* is creating disturbances in my room is definitely connected; I have no doubt of that. But I came to this house for Eleri, and if there's any child in need of releasing it's her. . .but," and she laid her hand on his arm. "I will think on it, I can promise you no more than that."

Tegid bowed his head.

"And that is all that I can hope for, Miss, but whilst you are indulging me, please allow me just one more thing. . ."

Beth waited.

"Have no fear of the gift, Miss. Have no fear and see it for the blessing that it is and allow yourself to be guided by it. Search beyond what you have been taught, look beyond the confines of what man has made of these things; seek only with your heart, and then, and only then, will you be at peace with what's inside you."

"You make a fine and persuasive argument, Tegid, I will give you that," she said lightly and smiled, "and have left me with much to mull over and mull over it I will. I'm just not sure I'm ready to start speaking to spirits, or if I ever will. But my thanks for your confidence in me and I promise I won't breathe a word. Come, let us join the others, I have a need to be around *living* people! "

As they made their way back into the copse where the two figures still dabbled their toes in the brook, Beth looked about her and suppressed a shiver as though unseen eyes watched her; eyes of long-ago gypsy folk who once laid claim to a beautiful white stallion. . .

Chapter 10

On arrival back at the house Eleri made it clear that she wanted to see the foal and that Nanny must come with her. After her talk with Tegid, Beth was keen to have some moments alone and hurried up to the nursery; her own room was the last place she wanted to be at that moment. To her great surprise she found Dr. Lewis lounging in one of the window seats flicking through one of Eleri's picture books and she came to a halt at the sight of him.

He smiled and stood up laying the book to one side.

"Sorry, I have startled you."

Beth gathered herself and gave an embarrassed laugh.

"Well, yes, just a little. Are you here for Eleri? She's just down in the stables with Nanny Gwyn looking at the foal, they shouldn't be too long."

"Then I shall wait, if that causes you no inconvenience?"

Beth shook her head. "No, not at all, Doctor."

It seemed incongruous addressing him as such for he still looked too young for such a title, and besides, were doctors usually this handsome? His eyes were warm upon her and she blushed.

You look a little flustered, Miss Watson," said the Doctor solicitously, "is there something bothering you?"

"Like what? I don't know what you mean!" Beth rejoined immediately and the hint of defensiveness in her tone saw the young doctor throw up his hands in mock surrender.

"Ah, I push too far, I see. I was merely enquiring for you seem a bit out of sorts, but then it cannot be easy working in such an environment as Galinas House. Forgive me, Miss Watson, I meant no offence."

Surprised at his candid remark Beth glanced out to the landing but decided to ignore it and coming forward untied her sun hat and placed it on the table.

"No, no, please don't apologise, I'm just a bit tired. It's been a lovely day, but a long one." She offered a tentative smile and he smiled in return.

"I hear you've been out picnicking on the moors; well, you've certainly had a fine day for it! And Eleri, how did my young patient enjoy her jaunt?"

Beth started for the second time in as many minutes. Was she mistaken? But did she not hear him call the child by her *given name?* She stared at him in consternation and he held her look innocently a small smile playing on his lips.

"*Emily* has had the most wonderful time; as far as I can tell, doctor," she replied carefully, "although I think Nanny Gwyn enjoyed it more, such was her delight at being able to dabble her toes in the brook. But we all enjoyed ourselves very much, thank you."

"We?" the young doctor raised an eyebrow.

"Tegid, he drove us there," said Beth with a rising sense of irritation. Why was he questioning her in this way? It was almost as though he was testing her, but for what possible reason? She moved away to the small bookshelf and pretended to reshuffle them into some kind of order as she gathered her thoughts.

"Sounds like fun. Perhaps you and your young charge would allow me the pleasure of taking you out on the next excursion."

She spun round wearing a slight frown and the young doctor chuckled softly.

"Why, Miss Watson, does my offer surprise you? I think it's an excellent chance for me to observe my patient in entirely different surroundings, which, as you yourself said, have had a favourable effect!"

"Well, I. . ." floundered Beth," I'm not sure that the mistress would approve, and besides, Nanny. . ."

The young man waved a hand.

"Oh, I'm sure Nanny could be persuaded to come along as chaperone, if that's what you're worried about, Miss

Watson, and as for the lady of the house; how can she object, when it will part of my treatment? But if it makes you feel any better I will gain the necessary blessing from Dr. Morgan *and* the Squire then we. . ." he broke off as Nanny entered the room with Eleri before her still clutching the sprig of wild flowers Teg had picked for her earlier.

"Why, Dr. Lewis, what a pleasure!" cried Nanny, "Look whose come to see you, *cariad!* Will you not say hello?"

Nobody expected the child to speak, of course, but still she astounded them all as she stepped towards the doctor and shyly offered him her flowers.

In the shocked silence that followed only the ticking of the mantle clock could be heard and then Dr. Lewis was bending down before her his face tender and reaching out he gently took the proffered posy.

'*Diolch yn fawr. . .*' he murmured evidently touched by the gesture.

Beth glanced at Nanny wide-eyed with delighted surprise and the old woman stared back at her, both hardly able to believe their eyes! Then Eleri stepped back and going to Nanny buried her face in her skirts.

"Well how honoured are *you!*" murmured Nanny in wonder as she stroked the child's head, "A sure sign of approval if I ever saw one!"

Dr. Lewis straightened up with a shrug but there was unconcealed pleasure in his face.

"I am very fortunate indeed; but then, this young lady is my favourite patient, I'll have you know, Nanny Gwyn!" he said with mock sternness, "Which brings me on to a proposal I was just discussing with Miss Watson here before your arrival, if I may be so bold!"

"You will be bold anyway, doctor, if I'm not mistaken!" laughed Nanny, "So what is it, what is this proposal then?"

"I would be honoured, if all ladies present would permit me to take us all out on the next jaunt, and as the patient has now experienced the delights of Gypsy's Hollow, I thought perhaps, a trip to your home-village and lunch at the Drover's Inn would be a step up. What say you, Nanny?"

The old lady clapped her hands in delight.

"I would say yes! Yes, please!" she turned to Beth her face shining, "Were we not saying the very same thing just earlier today?" But before Beth could make a reply she was bustling across the nursery, Eleri close on her heels.

"Miss Watson is less keen on the idea though, I'm afraid. . ." interjected the doctor smoothly and assumed an injured air.

Nanny Gwyn spun round and looked at Beth askance as even Eleri peeped out at her from behind Nanny's skirt and Beth squirmed uncomfortably.

"Well, no. . . I mean yes. I think it's a wonderful idea, I just don't think the mistress will approve and well, I. . ." she tailed off and looked at Nanny appealingly, "I do not need to spell it out, Nanny, because *you know. . .*"

The old nurse nodded.

"Leave it with me. The master will be home later today and I am sure he will raise no objection and besides. . ." she added with a mischievous glint, "he can deny his dear old nanny nothing!"

The next few days were busy for Beth, for in addition to her duties with the child there were also lessons with Teg on how to drive the trap. That meant extra time away from the house as they bumped their way across the moors, Eleri often sat between them, and soon the old man was satisfied with Beth's efforts and she was making regular excursions, even if it was just to the village and back.

Nanny's meeting with the master had gone well and Beth had been summoned so that he could thank her personally for the progress she was making.

"I am impressed that you have demonstrated such commitment, Miss Watson," he had told her, "and anything that can aid my niece in her recovery will be met with nothing but approbation from me." He added meaningfully, and Beth was grateful for his unspoken support.

"Nanny here also tells me that you have asked for instruction on how to drive the trap. That, too, meets with my approval. I have also met with both doctors who now feel such is Emily's progress that they need not attend quite so frequently, and that is a credit to you; and you, of course, Nanny." He gave his old nurse an affectionate look.

"Therefore, by way of reward and as a token of my gratitude I have put at your disposal the dog-cart that my wife used up until her. . . ill-health." His face flickered momentarily and Beth knew it was because there was actually nothing wrong with the mistress of the house. She had merely retreated to an idle existence spending much of the time in her rooms eating fancies and reading novellas.

"For theirs is not so much a marriage as a union of convenience," Nanny had confided to her one day, *"He has his heir. She believes she has done her duty and their arrangement is such that he is often away and she gets to do whatever she wants. There was a time when they would entertain, but since the child has come into the house, it as though a door has been closed on even that part of their life and it's actually quite sad really. They live almost as complete strangers now. . ."*

"The governess is the only one who uses it on occasion, I believe, but henceforth I have left instructions that it be primarily for your use, and your use only, Miss Watson. In future Miss Meacham can use the trap should she wish."

Beth glanced at Nanny who lowered her eyes demurely. That the old nurse had instigated the idea she had no doubt and inwardly she sighed for she knew how badly the governess would take this latest development.

She could hardly wait to tell her mother and at the first opportunity when Eleri was taking an afternoon nap she wrote a long and detailed letter outlining recent events, but fell short of including the ghostly happenings for fear her mother would be on the first train up agog to know more and witness the phenomena for herself.

And besides, things seemed to have calmed down. There had been the odd movement of items but not enough to warrant any further exploration, and so taken up was she with her everyday tasks she had pushed Teg's tale of tragedy firmly away from her until one night she woke to find the small figure of a boy stood at the end of the bed.

At first amidst the fog of sleep she thought it must be Eleri on one of her nocturnal visits, but then she felt movement beside her and reaching down she touched the small warm form of the child as she too, was roused from her slumbers and sat up. She must have slipped in whilst Beth was sleeping, a habit that was becoming increasingly regular. Not daring to take her eye off the still figure, Beth whispered, "Do you see it. . . do you see. . . *him,* Eleri?

She felt rather than saw the child nod her head, and they both stayed as still as stone as the slight luminescent figure stared back at them and Beth knew without a doubt that this was 'her ghost' and the tragic boy of Tegid's story.

As her eyes adjusted to the darkness his features began to take on more form, and she found herself looking into a sad little face with huge eyes that glowed beseechingly; a gentle face, a face so finely delicate that Beth could almost believe he was of the *Tylwyth Teg* from the nursery story books and her heart fluttered madly.

Her charge by comparison appeared strangely unmoved and she regarded the ghost steadily without the slightest trace of fear. As Beth's mind scrambled to make sense of what was happening it suddenly occurred to her that Eleri was not afraid *because she had seen the ghost before!*

As though he had read her thoughts the boy shifted his gaze away from Beth and looked directly at Eleri and there was a definite softening in the expression and the lips moved imperceptibly as though in greeting. The pale luminescence of his face was matched by the white nightdress he was wearing; he looked small and undersized and that only accentuated his look of *faerie* fragility.

But it was the profound sadness in his eyes that struck her to the core of her being, and remembering Teg's suggestion that she try to interact with him, she opened her mouth to speak but nothing came out, such was the intensity of the moment.

All she could do was stare as though in a trance as this lost little soul looked to her again and then began to fade slowly, as though being drawn back into the netherworld by unseen hands. The light around him grew fainter and fainter and then he was gone.

Beth released the breath she'd been holding and turning towards Eleri reached out and touched her arm. The child looked up at her, just a small oval of paleness in the dark, a strange glimmer in the dark eyes, but before Beth could say anything, her charge turned away and curling up in her customary sleep position was asleep within moments.

An owl gave a lonesome hoot somewhere outside and Beth lay back down her thoughts slowly settling like floating feathers around her.

So the story was true; all of it. Which meant that somewhere out on the moors a ghost horse did run; caught forever in a twilight world as the centuries crept by and life went on, their tragic tale passing into myth with just an old stableman who knew and bore witness.

Small wonder the ghost-boy had been trying to attract her attention and yet for what purpose? What did he want from her and how could she help him when the very thing he needed she denied within herself?

Her mind went back to how the ghost boy had looked at Eleri. The ease with which her charge had gone back to sleep as though nothing had happened. The complete lack fear or any indication of surprise, and Beth found this astounding. That this damaged little child should display such incredible indifference in the face of something so otherworldly; could it be possible that Eleri, too, had this gift? And if so, was this reason why Beth had been able to reach her more easily than had her predecessors?

It seemed to make sense.

Then there was Nanny Gwyn who had asserted on more than one occasion that she had not an ounce of anything mystical about her, and nor was she particularly interested. And yet she enjoyed a relationship with their charge on a par with herself; unless there was something Nanny wasn't telling her, of course...

As the owl called out again into the night, Beth realised that she couldn't ignore the situation any longer and that something powerful was at work. Either she could be swept along by what was unfolding, or else acknowledge that she had a part to play and work with the gift within her.

She closed her eyes and saw the desperate face of the boy before her.

"Hold on, little one, I am coming," she murmured, "I am coming for you..."

Chapter 11

The next morning was their day out to Nanny's home-village with Dr. Lewis, and as he had insisted them on driving himself, Tegid's services were not required and so Beth knew she would have to wait until later before she could speak with him.

It was a fine morning once the mists had lifted and Nanny was in high spirits. Beth had dressed Eleri in her best frock and had herself chosen a pale lemon gown that drew out the colour of her hair. The ghostly visitation of the night before was not far from her mind but this was Nanny's day, and a treat for Eleri and the last thing she wanted was to cast a pall with inappropriate enquiries.

Dr. Lewis pulled up smartly in the trap, his horse having been unsaddled and turned out in one of the paddocks for the day. He looked fresh, animated and handsome and Beth's heart skipped a beat.

As she went to get into the back with Eleri Nanny pushed her way forward saying, "No, Miss, you sit in the front with the fine, young doctor. Why would he want to sit with an old woman when he could have such loveliness next to him!" and Beth blushed furiously as the doctor offered her his hand.

"I must apologise for Nanny," Beth murmured as she took her seat feeling mortified.

"No need." Said Dr Lewis grinning as he pulled himself up next to her. "Nanny Gwyn is only ever really happy when she's in charge, and as this is her day as much as Eleri's we will indulge her for the sake of a peaceful trip!" And with that he took up the reins as Nanny muttered in mock protest behind him.

It was a jolly party that went across the moors as the doctor and Nanny bantered ceaselessly between them with Beth occasionally joining in. That they were acquainted well with each other was obvious, and there was much amusement as old village tales were revived and anecdotes laughed over, and Beth enjoyed their company immensely determined to enjoy the day.

Eleri sat quietly looking like a pretty little doll in a sea-green frock with a matching ribbon around her wide straw hat. There was colour in her cheeks and a brightness in the dark eyes as she took in their surroundings and Beth glanced back at her often, delighted to see her enjoyment.

"You have a great fondness for your patient, do you not?" the doctor asked after a lull in conversation. His tone was light and his voice low as Nanny pointed out the upcoming mountains to Eleri. "Is that wise?"

Beth looked at him taken aback and he shrugged.

"Just wondering, Miss Watson, and please, no need to bristle, I can feel your spikes from here!"

"Then why would you say such a thing?" returned Beth with a touch of asperity.

He laughed disarmingly and gave her a fleeting look.

"Because I like you, Miss Watson, and like our dearest Nanny, you have a tender heart and tender hearts can get broken. The child is coming on a long nicely but there will come a time, naturally, when your services will no doubt become redundant."

"How so?" said Beth feeling her cheeks starting to flame and he made an appeasing movement with his hand.

"Because nothing lasts forever, and sometimes it is better not to become attached to things. . . people in particular. The world has a way of changing, Miss Watson. I would not want you to be unduly hurt, is all. . ."

Beth turned in her seat and regarded him for some seconds.

"You know something, don't you, Dr Lewis? You have heard something and you are trying to warn me!" Her voice was low and vibrant with intensity and he dipped his head slightly.

"I know only that once the child is further along the lines of improvement and speaking; which we all have confidence she will eventually do; thanks to your excellent care!" he added hastily, but his eyes were as concerned as Beth's and she saw that beneath the apparent casualness of his tone, that he, too, cared for Eleri and that his intentions were good, "she will be sent away to school; there is a place in Cheltenham, apparently, that will provide her with an excellent education. . ."

He left the final statement in the air but Beth immediately understood the implication and the reasoning behind it. There would be no shared lessons in the main part of the house under the tutelage of the Miss Meacham, not if the mistress had anything to do with it, and Beth had no doubt that this decision would already have been made and insisted upon.

Her heart sank, slowly like a deadweight in her chest.

"I just thought you should know," murmured the doctor gently and she nodded stiffly.

Why she thought her position would be a permanent one, she could only put down to her naivety and lack of experience, and in view of how things stood in the house, of course Eleri would be sent away! Her presence was barely tolerated as it was. It was a bitter blow but she couldn't allow this development to mar the day as she forced a smile to her face as Nanny Gwyn called out in excitement.

They had reached the path as it rose and skirted the mountains as they left the moors behind and came into a craggy little village that spread out before them, all manner of houses and cottages constructed of the same grey stone and Nanny could barely contain her delight.

"Here we are! Here we are! *Edrycha,* Eleri, this is where I lived and played as a girl when I was *your age!* And there's the pond still, look, with the ducks!"

Their arrival along with Nanny's voluble joy had attracted attention and as the doctor stopped the trap outside the large inn a small crowd gathered and greeted both Nanny and the young doctor warmly.

"*Croeso nol*, Nan!" beamed one large woman, "how are things up at the big house?"

"Why, look at you, Emyr Lewis!" cried another, "you look more like a doctor than Doctor Morgan!" And there was much mirth. But amidst the banter all eyes were on Beth and the child as she shrank back before all these people and Beth assisted by Dr. Lewis climbed down from her seat and immediately took charge of Eleri so that Nanny Gwyn could engage with old friends without distraction.

Dr Lewis seeing how the child had retreated and was becoming overwhelmed hurried to usher them away from the curiosity of the crowd and into the inn.

It was a relief to step into the cool dim interior and a merry-eyed man in a pristine apron made a big fuss of showing them into the private dining room where they were greeted by two women.

"*Emyr!*" the older one exclaimed and swiftly coming across the room she enveloped him in a heartfelt hug. "Oh, how we miss seeing you! Don't we, Nia?"

The younger woman hugged him in turn. "We do indeed! You work far too hard, cousin, but I'm so pleased you are here at last!"

She turned and looked at Beth who she stood by uncertainly, Eleri pressed closely in behind her and the young woman gave them both a warm smile.

"You must be Miss Watson," she said and extended her hand, "I'm Nia, Emyr's cousin and this is my mother."

"Eluned!" the older woman interjected and holding out her hand went on, "let's not stand on ceremony for by the end of this luncheon we will all be friends, I know! Can I call you, Beth, or would you prefer Elizabeth?"

Somewhat taken aback by the forwardness of the introductions Beth was pleased nevertheless and giving the proffered hand a small shake replied, "Why, yes, of course, and Beth is fine, I'm. . . I'm very pleased to meet you both."

"And this," said Nia looking down at the half-hidden figure of Eleri, "is the beautiful Eleri *bach*, and this we know because Emyr has told us all about you, but then you are his favourite patient so that is to be expected!"

Dr Lewis gave Beth a sheepish smile and lifted his shoulders.

"Forgive the enthusiasm of my aunt and cousin, they are visiting here with friends and I could not miss the opportunity to see them and besides, they would never have forgiven me!"

"Indeed we would *not!*" cried Nia in mock indignation and then turning back to Beth she added earnestly, "You do not mind, do you? We just thought it would be lovely for everyone."

Beth liked her immediately; her honest eyes and pert, friendly manner and realised they were very much of an age.

"And so it is, thank you for thinking of us."

"Come, come, and let's get you all seated!" said Eluned taking charge, "I take it Nanny Gwyn will be here directly once she can get rid of the chattering magpies!" and she winked at Emyr who grinned in return and then there were more voices as Nanny came in accompanied by a wiry man who had a look of her about him and he greeted the two women cordially before Nanny Gwyn introduced him to Beth.

"This is my youngest brother, Iwan, I haven't seen him in at least two years so this really is turning out to be a treat!" declared Nanny happily.

Soon everyone was seated with Eleri between Beth and Dr. Lewis, and as the innkeeper and the maid brought in cold meats and cheeses and aromatic breads of all sizes straight from the oven. The men drank weak ale as the womenfolk' sipped tea, and there were fruits and cakes and lemonade for anyone who wanted it. As the atmosphere became lively as news was exchanged and gossip imparted,

Beth couldn't remember the last time she felt so relaxed and at ease.

The innkeeper's wife seeing how the child sat quietly at the table her eyes downcast brought in a basket full of kittens and soon Eleri was happily ensconced on a cushion in the corner as she played with them. and as Beth looked at the animated faces around her, she could almost wish the afternoon could last forever.

With the exception of herself and her charge, everyone knew each other, of course, coming from such a small village, and Nia, was particularly keen to make her acquaintance and they chatted easily about various subjects until her mother called a question across and then she found herself looking into the smiling eyes of Dr Lewis as he slipped into the vacated seat and asked, "Enjoying yourself?"

Nodding her head towards Eleri in the corner she replied, "Not as much as some."

They both gazed across for some moments as their charge cuddled a pretty tabby as another climbed steadily up the back of her dress. There was a look on Eleri's face that spoke of a quiet joy; it was extremely contained but it was happiness, nevertheless, and Beth wondered if she would be allowed a kitten, but the answer came as fast and as fleeting as the thought and her smile became tinged with sadness.

"My apologies if I upset you earlier," said Dr Lewis quietly, "I would never willingly lay any sorrow to your door, Miss Watson, but I thought it better for you to know. Please believe me when I say that my words were meant only with the best of intent.

Beth turned to face him.

"I do," she said simply, "but it leaves me with much conflict, I must confess." She tried to keep her expression impassive but the doctor's aunt was watching them with a small smile and Beth felt slightly uncomfortable beneath her scrutiny. She went on.

"For as much as I want Eleri to come out of herself and come back to us; by doing so and successfully, means then that I lose my position and which in turn means I lose her."

She gave him a level look. "Therefore, it is too late to warn against attachments, I'm afraid, for I am fastened as tight to that child as my heart will allow, and so I must bear the pain until the day comes when I am no longer needed. But at least I have a loving family who await me when it is my time to leave. Yet this poor little innocent, who has none other than those who are paid to take care of her, shall not be so fortunate, and the knowledge of that, grieves me deeply and is the hardest part of all to bear."

He studied her for some moments before giving a slight nod, and then reaching for his tankard said.

"Then I propose we give her as much happiness as is possible and let time do the rest, Miss Watson. However. . ." he swirled the ale in his cup and looked out innocently across the room, "professionally speaking, I believe it best we proceed carefully and with great stealth for sometimes it is not good to rush these things. Indeed in my foremost medical opinion it isn't good to rush these things at all."

Feeling a flush of pleasure at the implication of his words Beth felt ridiculously grateful and then catching the eye of his Aunt Eluned, knew that hers were shining and that the moment had not been missed!

All too soon it was time to depart and there was much ado as goodbyes were said and just the slightest resistance from Eleri to leave the kittens.

"They're old enough to leave their mam, Miss," said the innkeeper's wife kindly, "the child can take one with her if she wants."

"No, no. I'm afraid that is not possible," Beth broke in hastily, "now come, Eleri, they must go back to their mother."

Nanny Gwyn sidled up to her and said quietly.

"We can keep it with Teg in the stables. No one ever need know, they'll just think it's a stray that's wandered in.

I cannot bear to see her so disappointed and just look at that little face, oh *bechod!*"

Beth laughed despite herself.

"Oh Nan, you'd have us bring them all if you could. Very well, but we will have to be very careful. Here, she can have my shawl to wrap him in."

Eleri had already made her selection, it was the pretty tabby and she allowed Beth to wrap it up loosely before they all made their way outside as the groom brought the trap round.

After the final hugs, kisses and goodbyes, they were soon back out on the road as the day lent itself a golden light and it was a quieter, but no less pleasant journey as they crossed the moors with just the sound of the plodding hooves and the occasional call of a soaring meadow pitpit.

Beth looked back and smiled affectionately as she saw Nanny, child and kitten as they drowsed together, worn out by the excitement of the day their heads nodding sleepily in tandem with each other. And then she looked at the handsome profile of her travelling companion and knew the flutter in heart and what it meant and marvelled at the speed with which her feelings had grown before looking away in shame at her foolishness.

That the young doctor was attractive and what her mother would deem 'a catch' meant that doubtless he had many admirers and the fact he liked to flirt had not escaped her, for equally her mother also had much to say about what she called 'a cad' and had warned her daughter against the dangers of *pretty words that came from pretty mouths.*

But Beth had much of the stoicism and good sense of her father and recognised the need to nip such false hopes in the bud. She was an impoverished daughter of a preacher and a lady's maid; there was nothing she could offer other than an ambiguous 'gift' and a collection of books left to her by her father. And yet the young doctor had gone to such lengths to ensure that everyone had enjoyed the trip out, and it would be churlish to be ungrateful

"It has been a wonderful day," Beth said quietly, "Thank you."

Dr Lewis glanced at her and frowned playfully, "Why Miss Watson, you say it as though it has been anything but! Are you feeling unwell?"

Beth laughed softly so as not to wake the passengers in the back.

"Oh no, I am feeling quite well, thank you! I am merely a little distracted, I have much to concern me in the days ahead and many decisions that need to be made."

"Hmmm," murmured the young doctor thoughtfully, "sounds ominous, none that will involve you leaving us too soon, I hope, Miss Watson?"

Beth looked into the light brown eyes beneath the dark brows and saw only sincerity, and in a sudden moment of impulsiveness she wished she could speak openly and confide in him. But the feeling was gone as swiftly as it had come. For all of his friendliness and worldly manner even he would balk at ghostly tales and exploits more associated with a travelling fairground booth. Such disclosures would leave her not only open to ridicule but almost certain instant dismissal, and so looking down she smoothed her skirts and mustered a tone she hoped was reassuring.

"Forgive me, Dr Lewis, I make them sound more important than what they really are. It is nothing, really. . ." And she smiled disarmingly as her heart begged forgiveness, but if she was to go into the unknown, then surely God would understand that sometimes the light of a lie would keep her safer in the darkness than the full flame of truth?

Chapter 12

The next few weeks of summer passed for Beth and her charge in a haze of trips down to the stables and out on to the moors. Teg was as discreet as Nanny knew he would be, and took care of Eleri's kitten until it was big enough to find its own feet, and now that the foal had been turned out with its mother, many hours were spent simply sitting on the paddock fence enjoying the sun as the child found solace with her new friends.

"We'll have to give this kitten a name, you know, Eleri!" Nanny announced one day as she joined them outside. "I have a fancy for Taliesin; which means shining, or King, and he certainly is a handsome little fellow. What say you, Miss?"

"Taliesin sounds perfect!" Beth replied adding, "Or what about Taliesin *bach?* For I do not think he will grow to be a big cat, but he can still be a *King,* can he not, *cariad?*"

As she addressed the last part of the question to Eleri, she watched closely for a reaction and was rewarded with a faint quirk of the lips. Flashing a quick smile at Nanny, she said, "Taliesin it is, then! How's about Tali for short!"

They had both discovered a pathway to their charge that would open up when animals were involved, for she would positively blossom in their company and they in kind would be gentle with her as if they sensed her fragile state.

Both nurses, old and young, endeavoured to offer, present and appease in any way they believed could make a difference and slowly, gradually, all of their efforts met with small, sometimes miniscule, improvements every day. For in the light of what they had learned from Dr Lewis regarding Eleri's ultimate destination, they had discussed and decided that they would do what was best for the child, and that by continuing to draw her out of herself, they would give all the support that was needed but that reports of any improvements would be vague and ambiguous in the telling.

"I cannot say I'm happy having to deceive the master like this, for Lord knows he has been good to me" Nanny had said with a troubled brow, "but this decision to send the child away would not have come from him, I know, and the longer we can delay the inevitable the better; for my part, I owe her mother that at the very least!"

Having seen how distressed Nanny was over this particular development, Beth held her peace over her ghostly visitor not wanting to disturb her any more than was necessary, but she did seek out the old stableman at the earliest opportunity.

"And so you have seen him, then. . . *finally!*" Tegid had said once she had related the event and moving across to sit on the bench indicated she join him.

"Did he speak, this ghost-child? Did he say anything to you?"

Beth shook her head.

"No, but if his eyes could, such miseries I do believe I would have heard that night."

"Perhaps he is not strong enough," Teg said thoughtfully, "mayhap the energies around him need to be stronger. . . and the child saw him, too, you say?"

"I believe she did, but as I said, she was not afraid, not at all, which means. . ." Beth trailed off and waited as the old man stroked his moustaches before fixing her with a knowing stare.

"She has seen him before." he finished for her and then went on, "Yet not only that, she has seen him so often that his presence has become not only acceptable but usual to her which in turn leads me on to think. . ."

Now it was his turn to break off and he gave the young woman an intense look.

"That perhaps it isn't *you* that the ghost is interested in but *the child!*"

Beth drew back in surprise.

"Eleri! But why?"

Tegid pulled his pipe out from its customary place and tapped out the bowl smartly.

"Well, Miss, as the child still refuses to speak then that part of the mystery still remains with you, I'm afraid.."

A groom appeared from one of the stables leading a handsome chestnut and after tying it to one of the rings in the wall proceeded to brush its coat with wide sweeping movements. They watched him for some moments each with their thoughts before Tegid spoke again.

"Have you seen him since that night, Miss? Does he come to you often?".

"No, although things are still being moved around but not so much. Perhaps he has given up, perhaps he no longer feels I can help him; especially as it is as you say, that is Eleri he is interested in! Although what *she* could do for him, heaven knows, poor lamb!"

The old man's response was a long look and Beth threw her hands up into the air.

"Very well, I will speak with this. . . *spirit!* I would trouble you with one more question, however."

The old man waited.

"Nanny; I feel she knows more than she says, about the ghost-boy, I mean, and well, everything! I cannot help but wonder if she is sensitive to these things and yet chooses to ignore them. I would ask her directly but she has looked tired of late and I do not wish to put any more on her. But I have to ask the question; does she know?"

Tegid removed the pipe and put it in his pocket.

"All I will say, Miss, is that it isn't easy being a part of this household and Nanny, as you know, has been here a very long time. The master's marriage has never been an agreeable one and the family have always been . . . *tainted . . .* by some misfortune, or another."

"The gypsy curse," murmured Beth, and the old man nodded.

"Therefore needs must a person must protect themselves – including Nanny Gwyn."

Beth looked at him askance.

"I don't understand."

"You will." He said rising to his feet. "Now if you'll excuse me, Miss, I'd best attend to that clumsy oaf and show him how to pick a hoof properly before he takes the whole frog out! Just be mindful and stay alert and then God willing, the next time the ghost boy visits, let us pray he speaks! It all rests on that now, Miss, and so we must wait."

Beth was now eager to make contact. The whole intrigue of the situation had drawn her in and she actively looked for and yearned to see the spirit of the young boy, but there were only ever luminescent glimpses from the corner of her eye and a sense at times of being watched. There was still the odd movement of her possessions, but the ghost, to all intents and purposes, had pulled back and despite Beth's attempts to garner any information about him from Eleri met with lowered eyes and tightened-lips.

And so she threw herself into the weeks that followed as summer eased into autumn and bright, crisper mornings. There had been another trip out with Dr. Lewis only this time they had picnicked again out on the moors and had been joined by his Aunt Eluned and Nia.

Eleri continued to blossom slowly and would now shyly nod or gently shake her head when being addressed or asked a question. It was a huge leap forward but she remained mute and would curl in on herself if she felt overwhelmed by certain circumstances.

Her kitten, now growing fast and always happy to see her on her regular visits had now become so tame they would often take him out with them in the little dog-cart and Beth only wished Eleri could have him in the house, but it was too risky especially with Miss Meacham forever gliding about on her furtive patrols.

There was little contact between herself and the governess and great care was taken to ensure that her charge did not cross the path of her cousins as they haughtily went out about their business, but one day as she and the child trotted out from the village there was coming towards them four familiar figures.

They were approaching at a steady canter and suddenly overcome with a feeling of apprehension, Beth quickly bid Eleri to hide her cat beneath the blanket. As the child attempted to do so, Taliesin spooked by the sound of the hooves coming towards them managed to peep out just as they were passing and the boy catching sight of the wide frightened eyes wheeled round and came back for a closer look.

Instinctively Beth pulled on the reins and eased Meg to halt and looked up at the master's son as he gave a nasty chortle and pointed at Eleri's lap.

"Look, the bastard has a cat! She's riding about with a cat on her lap like a real-life witch!"

His sisters, drawn by the excitement in his voice also turned and trotted back to see for themselves as Miss Meacham called in a shrill voice for them to come away immediately!

With the exception of Clara, the youngest who glanced back governess guiltily, the remaining siblings ignored her calls as they stared in at Eleri their lips curling.

"Why, so she does!" The eldest sister cried in disdain.

Clara moved her pony closer and her face lit up.

"Oh look at the pretty markings! Is it yours?"

She addressed the question directly to Eleri and Beth was as shocked as were her siblings that not only had Eleri been acknowledged, but that she had been spoken to with respect and in a way that young children do when drawn by a common interest and everyone was stunned into silence for some moments.

It was broken as Miss Meacham pulled up her thin feature white with suppressed fury.

"Children, come away *at once!*" she cried and her eyes were on Beth as though she would strike her. For a heartbeat the young woman recoiled before rallying herself in a moment of defiance.

"No, it doesn't belong to anyone" said Beth pleasantly and ignoring the glare of the governess addressed the youngest girl directly, "it's just one of the cats from the stables that likes to take an occasional ride sometimes. Now if you'll excuse us, we'd best be getting back. Good day!" And as she gave a click to Meg they pulled off smoothly she could feel the stares behind her as they prickled all along her back.

"Well! I think it's disgraceful riding round the country like some, like some... *country cur!*" the boy shouted after them. Beth blanched but shook the reins firmly as Megan picked up the pace and soon they had pulled away.

"Oh look!" she said brightly to Eleri, as a flock of swallows swept across the sky in noisy formation, "they are moving off for the winter! I do so hope they all make it!"

It was her attempt at distraction, but the encounter had spoilt their outing and a heavy gloom had descended over them. As the cat crept back under the blanket and snuggled down to sleep, Eleri's head drooped like a wilting flower and Beth blinked back tears of frustration.

That there would be some kind of retaliation from this, she had no doubt; both from the mistress, ever ready to strike a blow, and a step backwards for her charge. But to her great surprise no summons was forthcoming, and within a day or two Eleri has returned to her semi-responsive state which led Nanny to make the comment that it would appear the child was either getting stronger, or else had become so accustomed to being insulted she had all but accepted it.

"No, no, sure not Nanny!" Beth had protested, "For we show her love and lots of it *every* day; therefore, let us view it as an inner strength, a sign, perhaps, that she is healing."

The old nurse had given Beth a knowing look but said nothing. She had not been in her position all these years and learnt nothing, and at the first opportunity she had quietly she had sought out Teg with words of warning.

But he, for all of his keen vigilance was thwarted, and one cold morning Eleri's little cat was found on the manure heap with its neck broken.

Chapter 13

The effect this had on Eleri was devastating and for the first time since taking up her role at Galinas House Beth saw her cry. Endlessly. Copiously. So beset by grief that Dr Lewis was sent for and he prescribed a sedative administered with warm honeyed milk.

As soon as the child had slipped into a deep sleep, Gwen was summoned to watch over her as the two nurses and the doctor went to Nanny's room to talk.

Nanny Gwyn was distraught, as was Beth, who knew all the months of hard work and progress disappear in one foul swoop, and they wept together for the child's grief in the knowledge that they could not assuage it, and may, God forbid, have lost her forever!

Dr Lewis was furious.

"Who on *earth* would do such a thing!" he demanded hotly as soon as they were safely in Nanny's rooms. "I cannot comprehend it! And yet it was a deliberate, I have no doubt of that and Tegid was more than sure! Have either of you *any* idea who could have done this?"

Nanny kept her face buried in her handkerchief but Beth met his stare before dropping her eyes.

"You do, do you not, Miss Watson? Or at the very least there is someone in mind whom you strongly suspect. . ."

Beth said nothing her heart torn between anger and a terrible sense of loss that all but threatened to overwhelm her. Never had she felt so hopeless, so wretched. She barely trusted herself to speak.

"Miss Watson!" barked the doctor and Nanny looked up in dismayed surprise.

"Emyr! Please! Do not take Miss Watson to task for what she cannot, *dare* not, say! Can you not see that?"

There followed an awkward silence broken only by the ticking clock as the young doctor gazed at Beth with a mixture of emotions as she raised her eyes briefly and then lowered them again.

"It is that young pup, isn't it?" he said in a low voice that reverberated with quiet fury. "It's the Squire's boy. He found out that the kitten was hers and sought to inflict more pain for no other reason than he's a nasty little monster and because he could!"

"Emyr!" gasped Nanny, and Beth looked up shocked.

"Oh, let's not bandy words here, Nanny!" he said impatiently "we all know he is a bad blood and with a cruel nature to match! His actions will now set my patient back in more ways than we could ever envisage; and what's worse is that we cannot prove it was him!"

He moved to the window and stood looking out tension evident in every line of his body as Beth and Nanny Gwyn exchanged worried looks.

He had never made any secret of how fond he was of Eleri, but his words and his actions now belied a deeper emotion, and recognising this Beth went across to him and touched his arm gently.

"She will recover, will she not, doctor? Please say that she will."

He turned to face her and there was still fury in his eyes.

"I'm afraid I don't have the answer to that, Miss Watson" he replied tightly, "for all we know the senseless act of this boy could have caused irreparable damage. But we will endeavour and we will do our best as we have always done, is that not so, Miss Watson?"

He gave a curt nod and then strode towards the door. The two women watched him, this kind young man as he wrestled to retain his mantle of professionalism amidst a rising storm of emotion. He placed his hand on the door handle and turned back, his face set the eyes smouldering and dark with purpose. He appeared to have reached some kind of inner decision.

"Squire Pritchard is in residence, I believe you mentioned earlier, Nanny?" His tone was clipped, his manner cold. Beth had never seen him like this before. Gone was the amiable, kind-hearted physician, and in his place a taut individual so diverse in his mien as to be a almost a stranger.

A look of horrified realisation came over Nanny's face and rising from her seat she cried, "Doctor! Emyr . . . *No!'*

"I'm afraid so, Nanny," he said firmly, "You may not be able to say anything, but I can! There is another sleeping draught should you need it and all going well, I shall be back on the morrow." And with that he was gone.

Beth went across to Nanny and taking her hands said anxiously,

"What is it? What is he going to do?"

The old woman lowered herself back down slowly and then slumped in the chair as though all the stuffing had come out of her.

"Probably the worst thing he could ever do. . ."

Still holding her hands Beth knelt before her and kneaded them gently.

"Come, Nan, he was angry, and the master is a kind man, surely he will understand. No decent father would condone such a cruel act."

"The Squire is also a very weak man," said Nanny Gwyn flatly "and one who won't hear a word against the children; especially the boy. He will not welcome our fine young doctor and words of recrimination, believe me; do not be surprised if it is Dr Morgan who will be attending in the morning."

Nanny's words filled Beth with misgivings, she had never seen the old nurse so hopeless. Releasing her hands she stood up and adopting a brisk tone said,

"Nanny, I want you to take some of the sleeping draught that the doctor left and go to your bed before you fall over with exhaustion! Then I'm going to fetch Eleri and carry her to my room where she will sleep with me. That is all we can do for tonight and that is all we need to do. Will you do this for me, please?"

The old woman emitted a heartfelt sigh.

"Very well, I won't deny I am in desperate need of some rest. What a day it's been, and an awful one at that . . ." she paused and gave Beth a quizzical look, "You know, *cariad*, watching you and the doctor earlier, you are not so dissimilar in nature and it was my thought that perhaps . . ."

"Nanny!" Beth intoned warningly and then swooping down pecked the old nurse gently on the cheek. "Now that's enough of that kind of talk. Here, I will prepare the draught for you and then perhaps the world will seem a little better for all of us in the morning!

Once the young woman was satisfied she'd done all she could for the old nurse, she went back upstairs and relieved Gwen who was wide-eyed and fretful.

"Oh Miss, I'm so glad you're here!" she whispered and glanced fearfully about the room. "There have been noises!"

"Calm yourself, Gwen," said Beth pertly, "it has been a bit of a day for all of us. No doubt it's just your mind playing tricks!"

She was aware that another untruth had just slipped out from her lips, but what else was there to do? The overwhelming distress of the child had obviously disturbed the ghost but why, Beth could only speculate. Her primary concern was Eleri at that moment and placing a hand on the maid's arm she said in softer tones.

"It's alright, Gwen, you go back downstairs, I will manage from here."

"Has the Doctor gone, then? Is the little miss going to be alright?" asked the maid, curiosity replacing fear now that Beth was here.

The young woman could well imagine the gossip below stairs and chose her words carefully.

"Yes, the doctor has just left and we shall have to wait to see how things stand in the morning. Thank you for staying here with her, Gwen, we are most grateful. *Nos da.*"

Gwen hesitated but then Beth turned away and going to the bed drew back the covers. Eleri was curled up tightly, tense even in sleep, and she moaned softly as Beth gathered her gently into her arms.

The child felt smaller and lighter as though the very life-force had been sucked out of her, and her little face, scrunched up with grief, was swollen and blotchy as though stricken with a pox. With great care Beth carried the sleeping form down the hallway to her room.

Gwen had opened the door for her on her way downstairs and soon Beth had the child tucked comfortably in the confines of her bed with a nightlight next to her should she wake up.

Darkness was moving in swiftly as Beth dropped exhausted into the window seat and looked out across the moors. She felt too tired to sleep; too overwrought.

She glanced across at Eleri and heard her slow steady breathing and dared to hope she would sleep through to the morning as she hoped, too, that Nanny Gwyn found the rest she so badly needed.

Her thoughts were in turmoil, her heart heavy with grief, and she looked out into the night until the stars came out and a crescent moon rose from behind the clouds until finally she felt her eyes start to close and thought she might sleep, when she heard it.

It was the softest of sighs and it came from just behind her.

She turned around slowly, her heart thumping, her scalp prickling, and then came face to face with the ghost boy.

They stared at each for some moments; the spirit figure gently oscillating as though caught in a breeze. And Beth; fascinated and yet awed by this other-worldly vision absorbed every tiny detail from the soft pearly skin to the feathery lightness of the pale eye-lashes even to the finely-weaved linen of his ghostly shift. He really was like a fairy being of myth, so delicate that if you blew hard enough he would scatter like seedlings of the dandelion flower, and truly she was captivated by him.

The eyes were deep pools of sorrow and in their dark depths Beth bore witness to lifetimes of suffering, as unfettered and free, souls came and went as this one remained trapped forever in an endless state of unrest.

He was so close she could have reached out and touched him. But there was an almost unspoken sanctity about his presence, and her hands remained in her lap as she sat motionless waiting for she knew not what, only that he had finally come to her and that she must wait.

The ghost-boy blinked slowly and then raised a thin hand and pointed across to where Eleri slumbered in a deep sleep and then pointed to himself.

Beth watched his movements closely in the understanding that there was something he wished to convey. He then shook his delicate head slowly before placing the pale fingers across his heart and then blew.

If Beth she thought she'd seen to the very dregs of this poor spirit's sorrow, the feelings that he put upon her now drew the breath out of her like wind through a whistle, and she gasped as all his agonies passed through her like a cold knife, and her mind teetered for a moment on the wave of such emotion she thought she might faint from the force of it. And then before she knew what she was doing she did reach out; unthinking, instinctively, her hand flew out and she touched the cold fabric of his shirt and could feel the frail bones beneath and raising her eyes slowly her heart skipped a beat as she saw the small lips opening and then he spoke.

Chapter 14

The young woman had no idea how a ghost's voice would sound, especially one that had remained silent for over four hundred years, and when it came her ears all but sang it as it weaved towards her like a high, reedy pipe as though coming from long way away, and tears sprang involuntarily to her eyes as she his small voice in it and her hand fell away from the ice of his arm her whole body overcome with emotion.

"Help!" he cried piteously, "Help . . . help us, please!"

Spellbound she watched as a tear slipped down the ghostly cheek as he stood wavering like a cold candle flame before her, a forlorn little figure, wracked with centuries of misery and despair and now knew why she had the gift and what it was for.

Reaching out and with all fear forgotten, she touched the cold fingers still pressed to his heart, and with infinite gentleness drew them into her hands and drawing him closer and in a voice filled with love, whispered; "Tell me, *cariad* . . . tell me what it is I must do. . ."

And in that strange whistling pitch he told her.

She remained in the window seat long after he'd gone and gazed out on to the moors and a world she now saw differently.

The experience had given a glimpse into a world that was *beyond* the world she thought she knew, and she marvelled at the enormity of it. There was much to think on. There would be no sleep tonight.

Pulling a shawl to her she wrapped herself up and kept vigil with the night as the child in the bed slept soundly on. Now that she knew what it was they had to do, the biggest challenge would be reaching through to Eleri.

She was the key; the *only* key and they didn't have much time.

The little ghost boy's face rose in her mind, the eyes deep and compelling, and Beth knew that she and Eleri would both need to draw on all of their faith and courage for the task ahead.

When Gwen came with hot water the next morning there was a barely suppressed air of excitement about her, and as bleary-eyed and as tired as Beth was, she drew her quietly into the corner for Eleri still slept and she did not want to disturb her.

"What is it? What's happened?".

"It is the master, Miss. In such a high temper we have never seen the like! He and the doctor had words last night and he has been banished from the house!"

"Banished! What, *the doctor?*" Beth could feel her eyes going wide.

"Yes, Miss. There was an almighty row apparently and the master is still fuming this morning."

Beth swallowed.

"Do you know what the argument was about, Gwen?"

Gwen leaned in conspiratorially and Beth felt a pulse of shame for tattling in corners like this but she had to *know!*

"Dr Lewis all but accused the master's son of murdering poor Tali and deliberately so to make upset for the child. Then he told the master *told him*, that the hate in this house for an innocent child was allowed to run unchecked and that if he ever wanted his niece to recover then he needed to take a firmer hand!"

Beth gasped.

"The doctor said *that!*"

Gwen nodded vigorously her eyes bright.

"Oh Gwen, *oh no*. . ." breathed Beth and thought for a moment she might cry.

"He'll not be allowed back in this house, not once the mistress gets wind of it. Such a shame, he was so good with the child, wasn't he, Miss? She'll miss him," the maid suddenly gave her a sly look, "although I'm sure she'll not be the only one . . ."

"We will *all* miss him, Gwen!" replied Beth recovering herself, "he was a very good doctor and yes, you're quite right, he was excellent with Eleri."

She turned away her heart heavy, for what this would mean for her charge she could only wonder. Dr Morgan was proficient, but he was gruff and behind the times; Eleri would never rally at the hand of his ministrations, but then such was her condition, would she ever rally again?

Her gaze travelled to the small shape still curled beneath the blankets and for the first time since taking up her role felt absolute despair. Then feeling was gone as soon as it came for there was much to do and she gathered herself together swiftly..

They had lost an ally and a friend, but there was still Nanny and Teg. Good, old, trusty and dependable Teg.

"Gwen," she said turning back, "would you please ask Nanny if I may bring the child down to her once she has woken. There is something I must do."

With a curious look Gwen nodded and then disappeared into the hall closing the door behind her. Beth washed and dressed as quietly as she could her mind now sharp as she shook off her fatigue. When Gwen returned with the breakfast tray Eleri had begun to stir.

"Nanny Gwyn says to come down when you're ready, Miss," said the maid, "and Cook has made some porridge with honey for the child, thought it might help."

"Thank you, Gwen, and thank Cook for me, please, she is very kind" Beth said gratefully, but Eleri would eat nothing and lay as inanimate and as lifeless as a doll her face pinched and swollen, her dark eyes flat and cold.

"Here, my *cariad,*" coaxed Beth, "then we will just bathe your face a little and perhaps try a little something later." And then wrapping her up in a blanket she carried her down to Nanny Gwyn who received them both gladly, and after settling the child down next to the fire, Nanny bustled across to her dresser.

"You run along now, Miss, and do what it is you need to do. I have some recipes passed down to me from my *Nain* that will help ease the grief." Beth saw her pull some small jars from the deepest drawer and seeing Beth's eyes upon them said,

"Only herbs, *bach,* no need to worry. Nature has a way of providing these things, and so first things first! You have somewhere to go, and I have some water to boil!"

Beth hesitated. She had never seen Nanny so agitated before and going across to her she laid a hand on her arm.

"Are you quite well, Nan? Did you manage to get some rest for you seem . . . restless . . . I can only assume you've heard the news from Gwen."

"That's yes to both questions, but please, don't let it get in the way of what needs doing," said the old nurse firmly, "you have your way of dealing with it and this is mine. But you can be sure we will speak more of this later and at least I have had the benefit of some sleep for you, poor love, look as though you have had none!"

"I. . . I could not. Not after. . . " Beth drew back just in time but Nanny wasn't listening. "I am just going to speak with Tegid, Nan, I will be as quick as I can."

"Take all the time you need," said Nanny pulling out a wooden bowl and pestle, "We will still be here."

Beth hurried down through the back stairs aware that her movements would be seen by the servants and speculated upon, but she knew they were sympathetic to her charge and so was not unduly worried.

As passed out of a side door to the kitchen gardens she made her way through the dewy grass and the gate that led to the stables. Teg was sat in his usual place in the yard as though he was expecting her, his feet stretched out as he puffed on his pipe seemingly content. There were sounds of activity within the stables as the grooms went about their business and the air was filled with the aroma of fresh hay and horses.

It was only as Beth drew near that she saw the pain in his face, and as she lowered herself down next to him he nodded briefly.

"How is the child? God willing she managed to find some sleep last night, although it's clear to me you did not."

"She slept right through, thankfully and is with Nanny Gwyn now. She is preparing some kind of tincture I think, to try and stimulate Eleri's appetite; she would not eat nor drink anything this morning."

Beth leaned her head against the wall of the barn and sighed deeply.

"Oh Teg, I know not where to start for things are happening so quickly and Nan and I are so worried for Eleri, although I know she is doing her best to hide it. Doctor Lewis has upset the Squire to the point he is no longer welcome in the house and I. . . I had another visit from the ghost boy last night. . ."

Teg removed the pipe out from his mouth and waited.

"He is more wretched than you can ever imagine, his fate is tied in with the ghost stallion much as you suspected, indeed they are so intertwined in their tragedy that one cannot be released without the other."

"But they can be released?"

The young woman drew in a deep breath, "Yes, but Eleri and I are going to need your help to do it."

"What did he say about Eleri? What part is she to play in all this?!

As Beth went to reply a yell came from one of the stables followed by an outraged whinny. She looked Teg in alarm as he rose to his feet with a speed that belied his years.

"How many *times!* That foolish boy!" he cried as a groom came hopping out of the stables yowling with pain.

"The master's hunter; I've lost count of the times I've told them to leave the feet to me! I will have to attend to the boy, to box his ears if nothing else!" He turned to Beth and in an undertone said, "The doctor left a message for you before he left last night; he asks that you meet him at the village inn between twelve and two today. He said will wait for you. I can drive you across if you are too tired."

"Thank you. I will speak with Nanny and all going well will see you here midday."

Beth hurried back through the gardens and into the house. Nanny had managed to get Eleri to drink some concoction and they were cuddled up together next to the fire as Nanny hummed a Welsh lullaby.

"All done?" she enquired.

"Not quite. . ." Beth hesitated, "I have been asked to meet with a *certain* person over in the village. Teg has offered to drive me."

"Then you must go," said Nanny and turned back to the fire, "we are fine here and as cosy as two fleas in a blanket, aren't we *cariad.* But there is one thing I need you to take care of, if you'd be so kind. I've had word Dr Morgan will be attending shortly and I would prefer it that we are not disturbed," her tone was light but the meaning unmistakable. "When he arrives, perhaps you would be so good as to tell him that the child is fast asleep and just apprise him of what is necessary."

"Yes, Nanny, of course," said Beth, "I will ensure neither of you are disturbed."

Dr. Morgan was slightly put-out when he came up to the nursery after what had probably been a difficult interview with the master, and he made no effort to hide his irritation when Beth told him that his patient was fast asleep with Nanny and that she didn't like to disturb them.

"I'm sorry to have wasted your time, Sir, but I'm sure you would agree that rest is probably the best thing for her under the current circumstances."

He grunted and made to leave before turning back suddenly.

"You don't believe that the girl's kitten was deliberately done away with, do you, Miss Watson?"

Beth was careful to keep her face neutral and lifted her shoulders slightly.

"I would not know, Sir, nor would I presume to offer an opinion."

He opened his bag and rummaged inside adding, "Well, you look as though you could benefit from some rest. Here," He held out a dark bottle and Beth took it from him, "Something to help you sleep, the child particularly, should she become hysterical. It has all been a most unfortunate business but we shall monitor her progress with the hope she will come to her senses or else . . ." he trailed off significantly and turned back to his bag.

"Or else what, Doctor? What do you mean?" The question was out before she knew it and he looked at her with surprise.

"Why, Miss Watson, surely it is obvious. The child's presence in the house continues to cause disruption, and if she fails to improve, then there will be little option other than to send her away somewhere she will receive the care she needs!"

A cold finger of fear ran along her spine as Beth understood his meaning. They were going to send her away to an institution! An asylum of some sorts! And there had she been fretting of the day when Eleri would be deemed well enough to be sent away to some kind of school!

The fate of her charge had suddenly become dark and more frightening than she could ever have imagined, and as the Doctor snapped his bag shut and turned to leave she dared ask another question and this time his response was sharp with rebuke.

"No, Miss Watson, Dr. Lewis will *not* be coming back! The child's care is in my hands now so I suggest you continue with your duties and leave all other considerations to me. Please be sure to tell Nanny Gwyn, I am sorry to have missed her but that I will come by again in a day or two."

And with that he was gone leaving in his wake a long dark shadow of despair as Beth fought back the tears that were forming.

"No, not now! *Don't you dare!*" she told herself fiercely and then taking a long breath she went to her room to get ready but there was fury in her heart.

Chapter 15

The morning was starting to cloud over as Beth made her way down to the stables at midday and it reflected her mood perfectly. She had said nothing to Nanny Gwyn, not as yet. Why not spare the old nurse and her charge at least one day of further heartbreak. Just when they believed matters couldn't get any worse . . .

As usual Meg was in the harness and as soon as they were up on the moors Beth turned to the old stableman and her manner was grim

"I'm afraid it is turning out to be something of a dark day for news, Tegid, for how can we help the dead when we can't even help the living!"

Startled the old man glanced at her and seeing his look she added.

"I assume you haven't heard."

Tegid wrinkled his brow, "No, Miss, what? I have no idea what it is you are talking about."

"It's Dr. Morgan. He has never empathised with Eleri not as Dr Lewis had, and now it would seem he wants nothing more to do with her at all. For he has somehow persuaded the Squire to lock the poor child away and the Squire, it would seem, has agreed!

If Tegid had been surprised before he was shocked now, for her anger was evident as her eyes blazed and shone with unshed tears, and reaching out he patted her hand uncertainly not knowing what to say.

"Oh Teg, they are going to *send her away*!" And then unable to hold back anymore the tears came flowing and the old man stopped the cart and awkwardly took her into his arms.

"There, there, *cariad,*" he murmured gently, *Oh bechod,* don't cry. . ." And his heart ached for this lovely, loving girl and the knowledge that time was now running out for that poor unwanted little child, and it was all he could do to hold back tears of his own.

Beth cried as she hadn't done since her father had passed away, stung into grief by the injustice of it all, overwhelmed by the emotions of both the child and the ghost, Nanny's attempts to put a brave face on it all, and for the cruel loss of an innocent creature!

Once she'd wept out all of her tears, she pulled away and dabbed at her eyes and took a series of deep breaths.

The old man sat back and stared out across the moors as she collected herself.

"Forgive me," she said quietly, "it all just . . . kind of . . . *came out.*"

"And so it needed to by the sounds of it, Miss, no need to apologise. Tell me, what does Nanny Gwyn have to say about all this?"

"Nanny doesn't know, not yet. I left her reading to Eleri when I left. They looked so peaceful I did not have the heart to broach yet more bad news. *Oh Dr Lewis, what have you done!"*

Tegid shook the reins and they moved off.

"You'll be able to ask him that question yourself, we'll be at the inn soon enough. And as for Nanny Gwyn; she's tougher than she looks, and you can be sure she will put up a fight to keep the child under her wing once she hears."

"Yes, but if the mistress has made the decision somehow I doubt that Nanny for all her persuasive skills will be able to win the master over on this one!" said Beth gloomily and Teg couldn't help but agree. It all looked so hopeless.

A fine mist had began to settle adding to the sombre mood when Tegid broached the subject of Beth's ghostly encounter.

"I'm sorry, Teg, how could I have forgotten, much less forget! I was just so taken aback by Dr. Morgan's disclosure I . . . I . . ."

He reached out and patted her hand.

"It is of no immediate matter and you can tell me on the way back. I have lived with the mystery and waited all these years, I'm sure I can wait a little longer . . . So let's just try and take all of this one step at a time, shall we, Miss?"

He smiled at her and nodded.

"Yes, of course, thank you, Teg. What would I do without you I do not know! I will tell you everything after I've heard what Dr Lewis has to say, for as you say, one step at a time."

Dr Lewis strode across the parlour of the inn as soon as they entered and took Beth's hands in his as his cousin Nia hovered concernedly at his elbow.

"*Thank you!* Thank you for coming! And Tegid, my thanks to you also; for your part, I have arranged ale and some fare at the back; I hear you and the ostler here are old friends" he said warmly.

"Aye, we are that," replied Teg, and satisfied that Beth was delivered safely he doffed his cap before making his way out to remove Meg and the trap to the stables.

The young doctor gazed at Beth with dismay.

"Oh, but you have been crying. Forgive me Miss Watson, for any distress my actions may have caused you. . ."

"Of course, your actions have distressed her!" retorted Nia pushing forward and took Beth into a warm embrace. "You poor thing, you look exhausted! Here, have a seat. Emyr insisted I accompany him; so there is no opportunity for gossip," she added meaningfully, "I expect that things have been awful up at the house."

"They always are!" interjected the doctor and then signalled to the innkeeper who eagerly came across.

They ordered soup that came with thick crusty bread and some ale, and once they had eaten Beth felt a bit better and in quiet tones related what Dr Morgan had told her and her fears for the child's future.

"You do well to worry, Miss Watson, for such an action will serve only hinder any progress she may make in her recovery," He sighed deeply and a sad look passed across the handsome features, "And if I am to be honest I confess I'm quite shocked that Squire Pritchard would even consider such a measure. It is so extreme! But then his anger when I raised my suspicions about the demise of the Eleri's kitten and the fact the perpetrator may be closer to home than he thought, elicited such a reaction, that had I not witnessed his anger for myself, I would not have believed he had it in him!"

Beth shifted uncomfortably, she was not at ease hearing the master being spoken of in this way, for the fear of someone overhearing as much for the fact he had never been anything but kind to her. But then, it was as the doctor said, for he was such a mild-mannered man that it practically defied belief that he should behave so forcefully.

"There is no chance of you coming back, then, Doctor Lewis?" she asked knowing the answer before he made his reply.

"It doesn't look that way, I'm afraid, Miss Watson," His tone was gentle, apologetic even. "The Squire informed me in no uncertain terms that he would suffer nobody under his roof who would cast such aspersions on the good character of his family, and that my services were no longer needed or welcome. Even when Miss Meacham was summoned and a more guilty air I have yet to see! But she denied any knowledge, of course, although she did confirm your encounter on the moors. She insisted the children had merely shown a curiosity, and an idle one at that."

"Their curiosity was anything but idle," Beth interjected, "except for the youngest child who strikes me as having a much kinder disposition than her siblings."

"Young Clara, yes, of all three she shows the most. . . potential," agreed the doctor, "but the governess was lying of course; but then she not dare do otherwise so beholden is she to the mistress I suppose she had little choice.."

There was note of pity in his voice, but Beth felt no sympathy for the cold-eyed woman who would allow a child in her care to commit such an act and then have the audacity to deny it.

"Squire Pritchard believed her, of course. He'd have believed anything rather than acknowledge he's raised a monster!"

"Emyr!" gasped his cousin and glanced about furtively, but besides a couple of old shepherds in the far corner chatting there was no one else about. The innkeeper was somewhere in the back berating some unfortunate for leaving the milk out uncovered, *yet again!*

"Forgive me," he murmured, "but it is not the first time that boy has invited my attention with his behaviour but you will just have to take my word on that. What matters now is the child, I am afraid that by being too honest with the Squire I have only inflamed matters, and for that I am deeply sorry."

He looked at Beth earnestly and she nodded imperceptibly.

"Word had also been sent out post-haste to Dr. Morgan soon after my departure, for he called upon me late last night and was far from pleased. But I am no longer a young apprentice and cared not for his tone." He made a rueful expression."So after a heated exchange I resigned on the spot and have no regrets for doing so. I told him that I would prefer not to attend such a family where cruelty and indifference was customary, and that I had not entered this profession to pander to the likes of Squire Pritchard and his son!"

Beth gasped and the two shepherds looked round. Nia sighed and shook her head for she had already heard the story and she gazed at her cousin with exasperated affection.

"So what will you do now?" asked Beth and the doctor gave a small shrug.

"Send out word, make some enquiries. We are fortunate, my cousin and I," and he smiled at Nia briefly, "that we come from an extremely large and close-knit family that extends from here across Merionethshire to the Llyn Peninsula, so I am confident that news of a position will reach me very soon."

Beth dipped her head hoping her sadness didn't show as the young doctor called out for the bill and then turning back to her said quietly

"But I wanted to see you to explain, and to apologise, of course, for I feel as though I have let all of you down; Eleri especially, but believe me when I say that if I have any regrets in all this is that I can no longer attend" he paused meaningfully, *"to any of you . . ."*

She looked away to cover her confusion and asked, "Would you like me to pass on any message to Nanny? She is quite heartbroken. Or some words, for the child, perhaps?"

"I would."

And reaching into his coat he withdrew a small white envelope.

"Please be so good as to see that Nanny gets this. It explains everything."

Beth took it and tucked it away in her skirt pocket.

"And for Eleri?" she asked and felt a ridiculous urge to cry.

The doctor fixed her with a sympathetic look. "Miss Watson, I know I am hardly in your good books at the moment, and I cannot say how grateful I am that you agreed to come and meet with me today, and if you'll allow me, I would like to presume just one more thing, just one, I promise!"

Beth swallowed.

"Go on,"

"That I can see you again, that you'll bring Eleri with you next time so I may say goodbye?"

He looked at her appealingly and she dropped her eyes so that he would not see the hope in them.

"You ask much," she said, "I would imagine I shall be forbidden to have any dealings with you henceforth, doctor, never mind Eleri."

"*Emyr,* please! You must call me Emyr now, for we are as friends, are we not?"

Beth looked at him in surprise and then to Nia who gave a small nod and smiled.

"Well, I. . yes, I suppose that would be. . . acceptable."

Or was it? She looked at the young doctor and his cousin who shared the same honey-brown eyes and saw only sincerity in them and besides Nan and Tegid, what other friends did she have?

"Thank you," she said quietly, "that means a lot . . . *Emyr.*"

It felt strange hearing his name on her tongue and yet comfortable in an odd way, and then they all laughed and it released the tension that had been holding sway over them and then looking nervously at her watch Beth said, "I need to get back. I told Nanny I would not be long."

As they all stood up Nia gave Beth another hug.

"Whatever happens I for one, feel as though I've found a true friend in you and it is my hope that you will stay in touch and visit often, should it please you."

"Why yes, it pleases me *very* much!" Beth then turned to the doctor who caught up her hand and gave it a slight squeeze.

"So you will consider it? You will meet with me again?"

Beth gazed into the handsome face and there was only one answer.

"I will try to arrange something with Nanny and get word to you somehow."

"Teg is very discreet and can be trusted," said the doctor knowingly and Beth's mind touched on the role he had played with Nanny and Eleri's mother and she nodded.

The mist had turned to a steady drizzle when they came out of the inn and Beth drew her cloak around her and over her bonnet. Tegid had already pulled the trap round and was waiting huddled in his coat, and after the final farewells they were soon on their way back across the moors.

"So how was your visit?" Teg asked.

"It went as well as could be expected under the circumstances." Beth kept her eyes ahead. "Emyr. . . the doctor, has requested we meet again so he can say goodbye to Eleri before he leaves. I agreed, despite knowing the risks. Once something has been arranged with Nanny, can I call on you to deliver the message?"

"You can," replied the old man, and then taking his old clay pipe out of his pocket he popped it into the corner of his mouth before adding, "and with my blessing. I have a lot of time for Emyr Lewis. He is a good doctor and a fine man, and forgive me for speaking plainly, Miss, but anyone can see how taken he is with you. Perhaps something good will come out of this whole sorry business after all."

"Tegid! What do you mean?"

"What do you think!" quipped the old man and she blushed and turned away.

"I think you have misread the situation, Teg," she said quietly, "we are merely friends as I am with his cousin, Nia. Our common interest is the child only, as it has always been, and now she will be even more heartbroken once she realises he will no longer be able to see him. Maybe I have been hasty in agreeing to a farewell meeting, perhaps it should be best left? Things have been happening so quickly I feel I am no sooner reeling from one crisis then it's on to the next!"

"Does this include your encounter with the ghost?"

Beth nodded.

"Yes, and we need to speak of this before we get back to the house. Tegid, I cannot tell you how incredible the experience was! I touched the ghost boy! *I touched a ghost!* And I was not afraid, not after that." she took a deep breath, "He told me how to lift the curse, he told me what it is we have to do and that I was to *ask the horse master for the magic words, ask the horse master for he will know. . ."*

She paused and looked at the old man hopefully.

"And so do you know the magic words, *do you know them, Tegid?*"

He rolled the pipe across his lips before making a reply.

"Aye," he said with a slow smile, "I reckon I do that." And her heart soared!

Chapter 16

As soon as they arrived back at the house, Beth hurried to Nanny Gwyn's quarters and was surprised to see Gwen sat awkwardly on the arm of the chair watching over Eleri as she slept. Beth removed her cloak as the maid pulled her into the corner, her freckled face twisted with concern.

"Nanny is down in the library with the master and mistress. They said you were to join them as soon as you came in," she whispered, "Neither looked too happy so prepare yourself for the worst!"

Beth's eyes looked beyond her to Eleri curled up beneath Nanny's knitted blanket.

"How has she been? Has she been sleeping all afternoon?"

"Just this past half hour or so, Miss," Then seeing Beth's look of consternation she squeezed her hand saying, "Don't worry, sleep is the best thing for her right now, and Nanny said she would cover for you, that she'd insisted you leave the house for some air."

The maid had a speculative look in her eye and it dawned on Beth in that moment that *all* of the servants knew she had met with the doctor, but then Gwen winked, "Don't fret, Miss, we're all on your side, your secret's safe with us!"

With a hollow feeling in her stomach, Beth smoothed her hair and gown as best she could and went down to the library and tapped on the door.

"Come in." Called the Squire's voice sounding more strident than usual and with no small sense of trepidation, Beth entered the room.

The master was stood in his customary place before the fire, arms behind his back an aggrieved look on his face. Nanny and the mistress were both seated on opposite sides of the fireplace like two queenly chess pieces about to do battle for the king.

The Squire's wife was swathed in a dark velvet wrap and had an air of satisfaction about her. Nanny in comparison was sat upright, her hands folded in her apron a look of tight disapproval on her face.

The Squire made a point of looking at his watch as he said, "Ah, there you are, Miss Watson! Back at last. We have been waiting for you."

Beth stood uncertainly just inside the door and then moved across to stand before the master her heart beating fast.

"My apologies, Sir, truly, had I known. . ."

"Never mind that, be seated." He waved an arm and Beth sat next to Nanny. She was aware of the mistress's eyes upon her and bowed her head before turning her attention back to the Squire. He was in an assertive mood. Never had she seen him with such a determined air since coming to the house, and she could only wonder at his wife's influence and what words had been said.

A huge fire blazed in the grate that cast leaping shadows into the gloom of the afternoon's fading light, and the atmosphere was ominous and charged with words unspoken.

The Squire cleared his throat self-consciously as though gearing himself for the task ahead, and then in a clear, firm tone he began.

"It has become apparent to me, in light of recent events, that Galinas House is no longer suitable for the needs of my niece, whom, it would appear is more afflicted than we had first thought. And so it on the advice of Dr Morgan, and with no small regret, that I have decided she will be moved to a place where her needs may be met more . . . *comprehensively.*"

As Nanny bridled beside her Beth felt her cheeks flame and the Squire held out a hand appeasingly displaying a glimpse of his former self.

"Please! Do not see this decision as any criticism of the care both of you have provided, for it has been nothing less than commendable. But there is the rest of the family to think about notwithstanding the smooth running of this house, and, in light of certain . . . *events*. "

A look of discomfort flitted across his face and Beth thought, *he knows!*

She could feel the eyes of the mistress on her but would not look for fear of what she might see in them, but she did reach out to Nanny Gwyn and take her hand. The old nurse gave it a tight squeeze.

"It is my belief that if the child is to improve then it is specialist care that she needs, and ultimately, as I'm sure you will agree, we must *all* do what is best for the child."

Everything seemed to be moving incredibly fast and despite this new air of assertiveness from the master, Beth could sense angst beneath his stern exterior and wondered what leverage his wife had brought to bear to bring about such a change of heart. And all for the callous killing of a kitten! It just didn't make sense. . .

In a voice that trembled just slightly Beth tendered the question, "How long, Sir, if you don't mind me asking? How long have we got before . . . *Emily* goes away?"

The Squire's face twitched and his voice softened momentarily.

"You have one month. It will take that long to put things into place, and although Nanny has asked for longer. . ." he paused and looked down to his wife who raised a languid eyebrow, "I am afraid that we cannot extend this any further, and so I suggest that you make the necessary preparations and continue with your duties for now. Suffice it is to say that your services will no longer be required at the end of this period, Miss Watson."

Beth bowed her head murmuring her thanks and then the Squires wife gave a polite affected cough.

"I believe there is nothing further to add, is there, husband?" Her eyes were alive with triumphant spite as she took in the dismay of the two women before her, and as the Squire shook his head and turned away she gave a smug smile and said, "You may go,"

Beth and Nanny Gwyn left the room with as much dignity as they could muster and knowing better than to speak until the sanctuary of Nanny's room, they held their peace until Gwen was relieved of her watch and they were alone. As Eleri slept on, they shared their disquiet in muted tones as Nanny dipped into her dresser and brought out a small bottle of brandy.

"I can think of no better time than now for something stronger; what say you?"

Beth nodded, her mind still reeling. Nanny looked fraught but there was a gimlet of a look in her eyes and two spots of colour rode high in her cheeks. That she was very angry, Beth had no doubt, but what could they do! The master had spoken. His wife had made sure of that.

"There was no gainsaying him, Lord knows I tried my best! But with the mistress there he dared not give even an inch of ground. It is probably just as well you missed the first part of that interview, *cariad,* for there were words exchanged that, for my part, could not remain unspoken."

"Oh Nanny! I hope you have not jeopardised your place in the house because of this?"

The old nurse drew herself up like a feisty bantam cock.

"No, no, you need not worry about that. I am as safe as I have ever been; I was with the family before *she* came, remember? He'll not have me pushed out and she knows better than to try!" Her indignant tone was replaced by one of sudden sadness. "But she has finally succeeded with Eleri and I will never forgive her for that!"

They both turned their eyes towards the sleeping child.

"How will we tell her?" asked Beth finally.

"We will not," replied Nanny firmly, "at least not yet." Her eyes took on a strange cast as they looked somewhere just over Beth's shoulder as though seeing something Beth could not. Her lips quirked slightly although as if in a smile Beth could not tell.

"What is it, Nanny? Are you feeling unwell?"

The old nurse returned her gaze to the young woman and then said something rather odd.

"I just wonder sometimes if God has a plan, and if so, why it is that it always seems to be the innocent who have to suffer."

"I know not, Nanny, although my father would say that everything God did was part of a greater plan and that it was not for us to question." She shrugged and looked away, "I'm sorry that as the daughter of a clergyman that I can come up with no better."

"But then you are no ordinary clergyman's daughter, are you, *cariad,* and who knows . . ." said Nanny as she pulled out two glasses, "maybe He has a plan for you!"

In the days that followed the two women did all they could to rouse the child from her stupor. Whereas before she had seemed to have merely retreated, now it appeared she had closed down completely, and she would sleep, deeply, with or without sedation, and when she was awake her beautiful dark eyes would stare out dully at the world and with no interest in what went on in it.

Beth had taken to bringing her to her bed every night and would tell her stories or just hold her tight. It felt as though her heart was slowly breaking, but there was nothing she could do other than offer what comfort she could, as Nanny too, resigned herself to the fact that they had lost her. Only Tegid held out a beacon of hope, and when he sent word to Beth that he would speak with her alone, he surprised her further by asking if he may come into the house.

Beth consulted with Nanny.

"Why does he want to speak to me here? He has specifically requested that he come to the nursery and that he would also like to see Eleri. Would that be allowed? What would the master say about it?"

"The master is away," said Nanny, "and the back stairs have ever served a more useful purpose than keeping the house staff out of sight. He is very fond of the child and has not seen her since all of this sorry business started. Send word that he may come, but to have his eyes out for that accursed governess; she seems to be everywhere at the moment!"

Miss Meacham, now that victory was in sight would drift into the nursery on some pretext or another, the thin lips smirking as she murmured false words of commiseration.

Both Nanny Gwyn and Beth were courteous but cool during these encounters and tried to ignore her obvious delight at their predicament.

As the afternoon was drawing in and the light fading fast after a dark rainy day, Tegid crept up the backstairs and was soon safely ensconced in the nursery when they knew that the governess was having tea with the children and the mistress.

He came in, holding his cap in one hand and a late autumn rose in the other. Beth led him over to where Eleri sat covered by a blanket as the rain tap-tapped on the windows, and as he went to hunker down Beth shook her head and fetched him a small stool. He accepted the seat gratefully, and then fixing her with a meaningful look he asked if might speak with the child alone.

Somewhat mystified Beth agreed and withdrew across to the hearth and threw more logs on the fire. She sat and held her hands out to the flames and watched intrigued as the old man leaned in to the child and began talking softly in Welsh, his voice rising and falling like a lilt of music on the wind as he held out the rose before her as though he was speaking of the flower itself.

Beth could not hear what he was saying, but his manner was earnest, appealing almost . . . *persuasive.*

The nursery clock ticked steadily on the mantle shelf as the minutes went by and the wind whispered softly and the rain pattered down and still the old man spoke. And then, as the light grew dimmer a pale shape appeared like the faintest mist and moved gently about them as though seeking to be seen, *or perhaps to speak?*

A ripple of excitement ran through Beth. It was the boy!

She watched entranced as he solidified and became clearer and then stood quietly beside Teg. He seemed to be listening and when he looked up as though feeling Beth's eyes on him he put his ghostly fingers to his lips and she nodded.

As Tegid drew back and rose from the stool the ghost boy disappeared in a whirl of light. Then Beth hurried over to him.

"Is all well? Is Eleri alright? Is she . . ."

"Sleeping, there's no need to fuss. Come," the old man took Beth's arm and drew her away before lowering his voice still further, he said, "You have always shown great trust in me, and now you must trust me more than ever, for time is running out and there will never be another chance like this again. Never . . . do you understand what it is I am saying?"

Beth's gaze returned to the child who she loved as her own and saw the small chest rising and falling, the rose on her lap like a forgotten keepsake and she nodded. "She sleeps, but it is a different sleep. And when she wakes, it will be a different awakening."

"What do you mean?" Beth asked concernedly, and the old man put a finger to his lips.

"Trust me, Miss. Trust me as you never have before. . . now please let us go and have *sgwrs* by the fire for my bones are not mean for such small seats and I will tell you now, what it is you have to do and the clock is ticking. . ."

Chapter 17

After Tegid had left the nursery and returned to the stables, Beth sat for some time staring into the flames before Nanny roused her from deep thought as she came in followed by Gwen with the tea tray.

"I thought we'd have tea up here for a change!" announced Nanny brightly and as soon as the maid had left, she went to check on Eleri before joining Beth at the fireside, the tea tray between them.

"Sleeping again," observed the old nurse worriedly, "I hope Tegid didn't wear her out. What did he say to her?"

Beth shook her head as she poured them both tea

"I know not, Nanny, only that he wished to speak to her alone and that he did so for some considerable time; he also brought her a rose. I'm amazed he was able to find her one this late in the year."

The young woman's attempts to distract the older one from the purpose of his visit were rewarded; however, when Nanny took her cup saying, "Knowing Teg he was speaking to her in his secret language,"

Beth looked at her askance the milk jug aloft. *"Secret language?"*

"Yes," said Nanny, "the one he uses for the horses. It's a gift passed down in his family, apparently. Not many have it, still less use it, although at one time it was common amongst the Welsh hill folk that tended to the ponies. It is called, *Y siarad-ysbryd,* but as I said not many have it now." She stirred her tea thoughtfully, "I'm surprised he even thought to use it, but then he's very fond of the child and wished only to help I'm sure. He is a good man, is Tegid."

"A good man indeed," murmured Beth wonderingly. Was there no end to the hidden talents of this man! He was like some kind of Merlin-like figure of legend and when

Eleri woke a short while later and was offered some milk, to both of their amazement, she accepted it.

"Why, Tegid's little chat must've worked, then, I'm thinking!" said Nanny delightedly, "Try some *cacen, cariad?*" And to their further delight the child took the small slice that was offered and began to chew it with a distant almost mechanical air and the two women looked at each other in astonishment.

But their happiness at this unexpected development was overshadowed by the sad knowledge that whatever improvements their charge showed now would not save her from what both regarded as 'her doom'.

"She will never get better in a place like that! Asylums are for mad people," Nanny had said with barely suppressed fury after their meeting. "If anything she will fade further into herself and be lost forever! Whatever is he thinking?"

And even though Beth shared her sentiments, she tried to soothe her, nevertheless.

"If it was left solely to him, he would not have made this decision; we both know this, Nan. Same as we know who it is who has brought considerable influence to bear. But what can we do?"

"Weak! *Weak!*" Nanny had hissed and Beth was taken aback by her fury. She had never seen Nanny so angry, and although she never spoke like that again, she went about the house with tightness in the once merry eyes and all who knew her knew the reason why.

It was as though the shadows that had always held sway over the house had become darker still and oppressive. But there was nothing else to do other than go about their duties in the time they had left and try and make their charge feel as loved and as comfortable as they could. Even the servants had adopted an injured air, and with the master now away on business from the house more than ever, the only happy voices in the house were those of the children as the days grew shorter, for hope had died with the long, golden days of summer.

It had also been decided, once Beth had consulted with Nanny, that Eleri was not be subjected to any further distress in the form of a farewell visit with Dr Lewis. Having got word to him via Tegid, Beth rode over on Hefina one day and had tea with him and his aunt in their well-appointed house that lay just outside the village.

"Less eyes and ears," remarked Nia who met her outside the inn so she could escort her to their address. "Thank you for coming, we have all been agog to know what has been going on and how you've been faring."

It was a muted visit, marred by the extreme turn of events and what it meant for Eleri, and once again the young doctor chastised himself for his hasty tongue.

"It would not have made any difference," said Beth, "there have been those bent on driving the child out of the house since she arrived, and even if you had held your peace, it is both mine and Nanny's belief that the outcome would have been the same."

The young doctor was barely comforted but both his aunt and cousin agreed with Beth that it was only a matter of time before those who were hostile to the child were successful.

"Yes, but what I also find hard to fathom is why Dr Morgan should be so supportive of this stance! He is, to all intents and purposes, a man of integrity – or so I thought! That he should be party to this cruel absurdity is beyond me and comes as a great surprise, I can tell you!" he'd risen and gone to stand at the window, his back to the room.

"Because he cannot deal with the child's condition," his aunt had replied quietly, "Because he has only ever known fevers and fractures and family ailments, and patients, who for the most part, will administer to themselves for lack of money and too much pride. The child's care is beyond him, Emyr, that is honestly my belief, and as the senior physician who has attended the family all his life, they would have been inclined to go with his opinion, for all of your best efforts, so please, do not blame yourself."

"And besides," offered Nia, "think of poor old Nanny Gwyn and how she must be feeling! I can imagine she is heartbroken at these turn of events as doubtless, you are, too, Beth." She reached across and patted Beth's hand affectionately, "and then when the poor child is taken away you will be returning to your family and I will lose a friend."

"You have all been extremely kind and hospitable, particularly in view of the fact that I am in service and merely a companion," Beth looked around gratefully, "Thank you, for making my time here all the more pleasant for your friendship," and turning to Nia added, "I will be sure to write to you and keep in touch."

"Please do!" the aunt said smiled warmly, "Emyr may soon be going off to pastures new but we will still be here."

"Oh?" Beth looked up at him and he turned back to the room before resuming his seat, his eyes still troubled.

Yes, I have been offered a position in Cricceth just over on the coast. The current doctor is well overdue for retirement and is keen that I take up the position quite quickly."

"How quickly?" Beth heard herself asking and then blushed, "Forgive me, I. . ."

"No, no, not at all!" said Emyr, "I will be leaving here in just under two weeks. Time enough to settle my affairs up here with Dr Morgan and say my goodbyes," he looked wistful, "Shame I could not have said goodbye to Eleri, but it would not be fair, I agree, especially as she appears to showing some signs of progress. No chance of the decision being reversed then, in view of her recent improvement?"

"No," returned Beth sadly, "I'm afraid that the Squire turned Nanny down flat when she made such a suggestion," She lowered her eyes so as not to show the pain still in them, "It would appear that he is resolved on the situation and that nothing will induce him otherwise. It is Nanny's hope that he may yet change his mind, but. . ." She lifted her shoulders and there followed a brief silence as each absorbed this statement and any last vestige of hope.

"I really must leave now," said Beth rising, "Thank for the tea, you have all been so kind but I had best get back to Nanny and Eleri."

When Beth's horse was brought round Emyr's bay was with it and as Beth looked at the young doctor askance, he said, "I'll not miss the opportunity to spend just a few minutes more in your company, and I thought I'd escort you at least part of the way, if you are agreeable, of course. Besides, it looks to me as though there is weather moving in." and before Beth knew it they were both in the saddle.

"Thank you, Ned," he said to the stable boy and then turning to Beth gave her his most winning smile.

"If you wish, but it really is not necessary," she muttered under her breath. Aunt Eluned and Nia were stood in the doorway and were beaming as they waved goodbye and Beth raised her hand in farewell rather embarrassed by all of the attention.

"Don't forget to write!" called Nia.

Soon they were out on the moors as a murky greyness descended and it began to drizzle. Pulling her travelling cloak more tightly about her Beth looked to the young doctor and gestured to the moorland.

"I doubt you will miss all this when you take up your new appointment. Although I am sure you will have sea-mists occasionally."

She tried to smile bravely. She would miss him, as she would miss everyone with whom she had become fond of, and her heart was heavy with the knowledge that this would be the last time she would see him, but at least she would be returning to a warm, loving home, unlike poor little Eleri.

"You are quite correct; miss this place I will not!" he replied, "A miserable, more depressing place you'd be hard put to find! I was brought up by the sea, in a place called Harlech, not far from Cricceth as the crow flies, so it is as though I am going home in a way and my parents will be pleased to have me closer to home."

"They are in Harlech still?" asked Beth and he nodded.

"My father is the physician there but he did not want me to have an easy passage into the world of medicine. Insisted I make my own way once I'd qualified, but he did put in a word with Dr Morgan, which is how I came to be here." He gave her a rueful look, "He's not too pleased at the circumstances under which I am leaving, but my mother will bring him round; she usually does!"

Beth smiled, "Then you are much like your mother, I would imagine."

"What, fearless, kind and persuasive? Yes, I think that she would agree with that!" and they both laughed.

"And you, Beth?" he asked, serious suddenly

"What about me?"

"Well, what will you do once you return to Brecon?"

Beth sighed and gave a small shrug.

"Look around for another position. The Squire has assured me he will tender a good reference, and so I will see what is out there and then venture forth. What else is there for someone like me?"

"Marry a doctor, perhaps?"

She pulled on the reins bringing Hefina to a sudden stop and stared at him.

He'd also reined in and sat looking calmly out into the mist as though he'd just made some banal remark about the weather. Then he turned and looked directly at her his features alight with hope.

"If you would have him, of course. . ."

She continued to gaze at him stunned disbelief for some moments before finding her voice.

"You mean to say, that you would have *me? As a wife!*"

He threw back his head and laughed, "Why, Beth, you make it sound as though the idea is preposterous!"

"Well, that's because it is!" she retorted hotly, "I have *nothing*, I am nothing, I . . ."

"You are *everything!*" he broke in with equal passion, "You are *everything* to me and *everything* I would seek in a wife; brave, beautiful, clever, and with a heart so full of love a man would never starve for want of it. And . . ." he leaned forward in the saddle, "as if all that wasn't enough, you would also make an excellent doctor's wife!"

As his words hovered in the mist between them, Beth stared into the handsome face was struck dumb with amazement. She was aware of a shout in the distance but his eyes were warm upon her and her heart was in her mouth.

" I've fallen in love with you, Beth, it really is as simple as that, and I cannot let you go without knowing if you feel the same."

The shout came again closer now and peering ahead Beth saw a familiar figure approaching and knew it to be Teg. He was in the dog-cart, Meg's little legs a white blur in the mist and she realised that he'd come looking for her.

"And so do you . . . *do you, Beth?*" his tone was urgent and Beth turned away.

"You have taken me much by surprise, Emyr . . . I. . . I need time to think,"

"And time you shall have, *fy nghariad.*" he murmured and her eyes widened at the term of endearment before Teg pulled up and looked in concern from one to the other. "What's happened?" he said pointedly, "is everything *iawn?*"

"Everything is fine, Teg, don't look so worried!" countered Emyr and with a meaningful look at Beth added, "Or at least I hope it will be."

He doffed his hat.

"I was going to escort Miss Watson back to the house, but as you have appeared through the mist once again like the knight *parfait* I will now pass this fair maiden over into your safe hands, Tegid, and wish you God speed on your return journey! The mist is getting thicker by the minute so I will not delay you a minute longer," and then bringing his horse close in to Beth's, he lifted her gloved hand and kissed it.

"I hope this is not goodbye; I will await your answer," and then with a flourish of his cloak he nodded to Teg's bewildered face before taking off back down the path until all that could be heard was the faint echo of hooves.

Beth gazed at the hand he had kissed and the lifted her eyes slowly to Teg.

"Well!" he said and shook his head slowly, "Was that what I just think it was? Has the good doctor asked for your hand in marriage, then, Miss?"

"Yes, Teg, yes, he has. . ." and she searched the old face for disapproval and found only an expression of delight.

"At last some *happy news!* And so what did you say, Miss? Will you accept?"

He looked at her eagerly and she realised that this was something he'd been hoping for, albeit secretly for some time, and she wondered if Nanny and half of the servants were in on it, too. The languid face of the mistress rose up before her as did the cold features of the governess, and well she could imagine what they would say and the swiftness with which she would be despatched from the house.

But then what about her? How did she feel about it? That he was attractive and that she found him exciting wasn't in doubt. But his passion also unnerved her a little as did his supreme self-confidence and belief that he was always right, for Beth was not of a malleable nature and could rise quickly in ire like the rest. It would make for a tempestuous marriage.

And then there was her status that was little more than menial; the daughter of a humble clergy man and a lady's maid. Hardly fitting material for a doctor's wife!

Inwardly she smiled at her folly for even believing for just one second that she could consider marrying someone so much better than herself. It was flattering that he had asked her, certainly, but it was a wistful dream and no more substantial than the mist on the moor and so turning to Tegid she said lightly, "No, I think not, but it was an honour that he considered me."

As they made their way back to Galinas House, the old man said no more about it but he could not help but feel a deep disappointment. Such a lovely young couple, so well-matched, how could she have turned him down! He couldn't comprehend it.

"What is it, Teg?" asked Beth concernedly, "You seem morose. I take it we are still on course for the task ahead of us? It has come up upon us so quickly I can scarce believe it, just a few more days; my heart beats so fast every time I think of it."

Aye, but not for the doctor, Teg almost said but kept his peace.

"Yes, Miss, have no doubt we are still on course," he said gravely, "Have the child ready and I will come for you at the appointed time. . ."

Chapter 18

It was just a couple of days later when Nanny found out about Emyr's proposal. Tegid had made sure of that and the old nurse was far from pleased and not a little hurt when she went to Beth for confirmation.

"What I cannot understand is why you did not tell *me!*"We have been through so much, *cariad*, shared so much, I thought I would have been the first one to be brought into your confidence, *not Teg!"*

Beth was dismayed, "Oh Nanny, I'm so sorry but it wasn't like that. When Tegid came upon us on the moor Emyr saw fit to kiss my hand in front of him which left him in no doubt as to his intentions, and it was nothing more than that, I swear."

"Oh, so he is serious then?" Nanny said with a touch of asperity, "and yet you still not see fit to share this news with me! And what's worse, is that you have *refused him*, I hear!"

By now Nanny Gwyn was openly bristling and laying a hand on her arm Beth said earnestly, "Nan, I said nothing because I *knew* what you would say. . ."

"And what would that be?" Nanny retorted tartly, "That you would not find a better match? Or that it's quite obvious to everyone that *he adores you!* Or that there are few opportunities, not to mention proposals worth having when you are in service *and yet you turned down a doctor,* and a mighty fine-looking fellow at that, o*h cariad!"*

Beth remained stoic as she gave her reasons. She was not worthy, it was too good a match for her, their acquaintance hadn't been long enough, and then of course, there was the fact that her gift made her different; but she was careful not to mention that!

Nanny merely huffed and pursed her lips before bustling off muttering to herself. Beth was sorry she had hurt the old nurse's feelings, but she had made her decision and would not even mention it to her mother in anticipation of garnering the same response.

Beth's primary concern was Eleri and every night she would take her to her bed and if this act was now common knowledge throughout the house, nobody passed comment, for what did it matter now in the time that was left, and for Beth, the days were passing too quickly.

Autumn was well and now truly upon them with chill, misty mornings and crunchy leaves underfoot. Eleri no longer wanted to visit the stables. She would resist with a grimace of distress and Beth did not push her. But she would allow herself to be wrapped up and led down to the gardens where they would sit for short periods and feed crumbs Cook had kindly provided for the birds.

As the season was dying it was as though everything was starting to fade and Beth would rise in the mornings with a feeling of hopelessness that was further enhanced by the ever-louring gloom of the house.

The ghost of the young boy remained hidden but watching, and when she and Eleri snuggled down beneath the covers at night she sensed he was not far and kept vigil as they slept. It was a strangely comforting thought, but then he had good reason. She had made him a promise and as the appointed day was now nearly upon them it was time to let the child in on the secret.

The morning before after they'd had breakfast and were sat in the window of Beth's bedroom, she took Eleri's tiny hands in hers and rubbed them gently as the child gazed unseeing out across the moors.

"Eleri, there is something I need to tell you, to share with you . . . like a secret." she paused for it *was* a secret; not even Nanny Gwyn knew about it and she felt a twinge of guilt, but Teg had been firm in his instruction; not a word to anyone!

"Do you remember that first day when we met down in the garden, and I said that we could be like sisters?"

Intently she looked for any kind of response, but the eyes remained empty and nothing stirred.

"Well, sisters have secrets because they trust for one another, and you trust me, *cariad,* do you not?"

Beth kissed the cold fingers. There was no reply but she knew the child was listening.

"As we know there is the ghost of a little boy in this house that has been here a very, very long time and he is so terribly sad because he cannot leave. And so when he comes to visit us, it has been to ask for our help . . . but then I think you already know this, *cariad,* for it is my belief that often he has come to you."

Now there was something; just the faintest twitch. Beth plunged on.

"He has a special friend that waits for him out on the moors and they are desperate to be together. But there is something that binds them and keeps them apart; something that happened a long time ago."

Beth paused. What she was about to ask of the child was phenomenal in both terms of belief and the trust that Eleri had for her. Indeed it was almost too much, but the old man had insisted.

"It will also help the child," he had said urgently, "I know you cannot see it now, Miss, but it all ties together and it is their only chance; it is her *only* chance!"

Beth wasn't sure what he meant and he refused to say more. But what she did know was that she trusted *him,* and if anything could be gained from this that would help Eleri then she would take it with both hands, and gladly.

"You have been through so much, Eleri, and I would never do anything that would hurt you or harm you in *any* way . . . but if we are help this young boy break the curse forever, then there is only way and I must have your trust like never before . . ."

She leaned forward and whispered in the child's ear before placing a soft kiss onto the smooth forehead.

"I love you." she said simply, "I love you with all of my heart as if you were my own, and I would never ask such a thing if there was some other way . . . but if old Tegid is right; that by helping the ghost boy means helping *you*, then I believe we have to try with the hope there is still enough good in this world to make magic happen . . So what do you say, Eleri, are you willing to do this thing."

Beth held her breath and waited.

With infinite slowness Eleri turned her head and raised her dark eyes to Beth's face. The blank look had gone and in their place a strange intensity burned deep within their depths and then the small chin lifted and then dipped.

She would do it!

Chapter 19

Beth did not realise it but that morning was her last at Galinas House. The rest of the day passed slowly and the greyness of the skies added to the overall mood of gloom and by midday a steady drizzle had set in that blanketed the moors and swathed the house in a damp oppressive air.

Once lunch was over Beth did not have to insist that Eleri have a nap, for the child, ever ready to lose herself in slumber fell asleep quickly as Beth tucked her in against the chill that seemed to pervade every corner of her room.

Throwing several more logs on to the fire, Beth then retired to the window seat with her book and pulled a wrap around her for extra warmth. Soon she was immersed in the story of Branwen and how she was saved by the birds when she was roused by a gentle tap on the door.

It was Nanny Gwyn.

"Such a cold and miserable day to be sat reading Welsh folk tales when you could have a *panad* with me," she whispered across and then looked at the sleeping form of Eleri, "she will sleep a while longer, no doubt. Come, *cariad,* it's warmer in my room.

Beth needed no further persuading and after satisfying herself that Eleri was as in a deep sleep as only those seeking solace would know, she soon found herself settled in next Nanny's roaring hearth with a cup of hot tea.

"You seem a bit. . . distant today, *cariad,"* Nanny said as she stirred in some sugar but her eyes were on Beth and she was worried, "it has been a troubling time, I know, but are you feeling quite well?"

Careful to keep her gaze on the flames for fear the canny old woman would see the secrets within her, Beth nodded.

"Yes, thank you, just tired is all, Nanny. It has been, as you say, a difficult time."

She felt awful hiding the truth, but things were so far along now that any enlightenment or confessions would have to wait. But then she wasn't entirely being dishonest for she *was* tired! Heart-sick of seeing a poor innocent child penalised for the sins of her parents; worn down by the endless spite of a fellow-servant whose ill-will was actively fostered in the young minds she tutored; and weary of being at the whim of a spoilt and selfish woman whose merciless machinations to banish her husband's kin had finally won out, and would likely prove to be the death-knell of her poor innocent charge.

As though reading her thoughts, Nanny rose and leaving her armchair, came and sat next to Beth so that the young woman had no other choice than to look at her.

"It has been an extremely trying time for you, I know. But then life in service and for people like us the path is rarely smooth. But when you go from here, try to take all of the happy times as well; the nice moments, the achievements, *cariad"*

The old nurse peered at her closely but Beth was careful to keep her expression neutral.

"It has been a lot to carry for one so young, and yet you have shown such strength of character I could only have dreamed about when I was your age. And even now, as I see how events in this house have sapped you. . . I see also how it has made you; and made you stronger still. Does that make sense to you?"

Beth struggled to retain a passive air as the thought came to her that Nanny knew *something!* But she saw only concerned affection in the faded blue eyes and inwardly chastised herself for being so fanciful.

It is the guilt, she thought, and then nodded stiffly as her lips struggled to form a smile.

"And it is by being strong that we find our place in this world, and that by doing so we show our true worth," Nanny went on and then squeezed her hand, "Never feel regret for coming here. . . regret nothing, for it is my belief that God has a plan for everything. . ." and as Beth's eyes widened, she patted her hand before resuming her seat adding, "but then, what would I know, for He never discusses these things with me; what will be, will be."

Nanny's words reverberated around Beth's head long after she had returned to room to find that Eleri was still sleeping.

What will be, will be. . .

Did Nanny know something she didn't? But to have enquired further would have been to betray herself and so she'd said nothing as Nanny went on to talk of other things as though that odd segment of their conversation had never happened.

She had declined Nanny's usual offer of supper in her rooms, insisting that a few more logs on the fire was all that was needed in hers, and that she'd planned an early night with just her and the child and a tale from the Mabinogion. But to ensure the old nurse didn't fret, she had more wood brought up and settled down for the evening.

Eleri, when she woke, partook only of some soup and a little bread and once Gwen cleared the trays, Beth and the child curled up on the bed and soon Eleri was drowsing in the crook of her arm.

Beth let her sleep, it would time enough to rouse her and get her up.

The hours crawled by measured by the ticking of the small clock as Beth read quietly. Her eyes merely skimmed the words and her thoughts kept flitting out to the moors as an owl gave an occasional screech and somewhere deep in the house someone slammed a door loudly.

And then just before midnight, Beth stirred and gently woke the child who blinked at her sleepily as Beth whispered that the time had come.

Quietly she pulled out the extra warm clothing she had taken from Eleri's chest earlier and hidden in hers, and once she'd added some layers and a thick, woollen cloak, she did the same for herself, and then taking the child by the hand she led her from the room.

"We must be as quiet as the quietest of mice," she had breathed to Eleri, "this old house creaks as you know and we must be extra careful not to wake Nanny when we go past her door, alright, *cariad?*"

The dark eyes of the child had merely looked at her but Beth knew she understood, and placing a kiss on the pale forehead she said, "You are the bravest and most beautiful little girl I have ever known, and your mother would be so proud of you this night, as would your father. Come, it is time . . ."

Creeping down the darkened stairs they made their way carefully along the landing without a sound and were soon descending the backstairs that led to the kitchens and outside. At the doorway that led to the herb garden a dark figure moved and Beth clutched at the child instinctively.

"Iawn, iawn, it's only me," murmured the unmistakable voice of Teg and Beth let her breath loose in a low rush. Eleri huddled in next to her as the old man came forward and hunkered down before her.

In soft but rapid Welsh he whispered something to her, and Beth felt rather than saw the child nod her head. And then straightening up, Tegid produced a lantern with a muted light and said, "Are you ready, Miss?"

"As I'll ever be! Lead on."

The old stableman led the way past the kitchen gardens and through the small gate that led out on to the moors. A bloated moon seemed to sail across the sky the swirling mist as its sea, and the chill air pressed around them like a living thing. Beth shivered, her whole being thrumming with anticipation and she kept Eleri close.

Somewhere close by an owl hooted as though announcing their arrival as they trudged in silence away from the house going deeper on to the moor like three pilgrims intent on their task, and soon they were swallowed up by the mist.

Looking back Beth could see Galinas House sat like a dark malignant spider as it watched them draw further away and she suppressed another shiver as though unseen eyes watched their progress with malevolent intent.

She frowned and swept her gaze forward as the old man ambled purposely ahead, the lamp held before him like some kind of talisman and the tendrils of mist gave before him like questing fingers seeking the light.

A large twisted form rose up ahead and Tegid made his way unfailingly towards it, glancing back briefly to ensure his companions were still behind him. No words were spoken. Not even a whisper of reassurance. And as Beth looked down at the small hooded figure beside her heart swelled with love and she squeezed the cold fingers encouragingly, for the child had kept pace and without complaint.

Tegid came to a halt just before the corpse of what had once been a sturdy tree and turned to face them.

His face was set, although a realm of emotions surged beneath the surface betrayed by the odd glow in his eyes that now surveyed them as he held up the lamp.

"We are here." He said simply but his voice was hoarse, and looking beyond him Beth took in the scarred and battered trunk and knew it to be the place where once, some four hundred years ago, an innocent beast fought and lost its life on the whim of a vain and vengeful man.

Her gaze returned to Teg and he nodded.

"What do we do now?" she asked drawing the child in close to her.

"We wait." He said and carefully placed the lamp on the ground.

The silence drew out as they stood motionless, eyes searching the mist; the atmosphere so eerie it was as though the moors had eyes and that it was *aware.*

A low noise began, as though deep beneath the earth, and Beth looked anxiously to the old man whose face answered her question as the sound grew louder and the very ground seemed to shake. It drummed and it rumbled and grew louder still, becoming thunderous as though something huge and unstoppable was coming at great speed and Beth clutched the child even tighter to her as Eleri let out a soft moan that might have been fear.

The thundering grew greater and was all but upon them when suddenly something erupted from the earth with all the fury of an elemental force, and then rising up before them as it lunged towards the skies was the ghost-horse of legend, the beast of Galinas moor and Tegid moaned as he fell to his knees tears running down his face!

Beth watched frozen to the spot as the beast tossed its great head and emitted a piercing cry. She could feel Eleri's face pressed tightly against her as the small shoulders hunched against the sound, and for one flashing moment Beth thought, "What have I done! *Dear God, what have I done!*"

And then the creature was away! With a cacophony of its massive hooves, the ghost-horse charged off into the night, a white blur of mane and tail that rippled like banners as a huge chain whipped behind it bound forever around its neck. It screamed and it called and the awful sounds tore into the night as the beast plunged and kicked and screeched its fury like some demonic being released from the very bowels of hell itself!

The very air seemed to vibrate with wrath as even the moon hid itself behind a wisp of cloud as the creature raged and the chains flew about its neck, and then rearing up impossibly high, its front legs plunged against the sky before dropping down to tear wildly at the ground in frenzied despair.

Beth felt tears on her face and looked wildly to Tegid but he was still on his knees his face frozen in anguish. And then the creature was coming straight towards them, and she gasped and turned to shield the child, her eyes squeezed tight and with such terror in her heart she thought she would die on the spot!

The thundering hooves drew nearer like a portent of doom that all but threatened to overwhelm her and she felt a sob rise in her throat. The enraged spirit of the stallion was almost upon them, and then there was silence.

Slowly she turned and felt her eyes widen as the great white beast stood not five paces from where she stood.

She sensed rather than saw Tegid rise painfully to his feet for she didn't dare take her eyes off the beast.

"Keep still, I beg of you. *Do . . . not . . . move!*"

She heard Tegid's voice as though it was coming from a thousand miles away, and then he was next to her and she could've wept!

The ghost-horse blew and its pale flanks heaved as it regarded the two figures intently, ears pricked forward, its tail softly blowing in an unseen breeze. The chains that were its torment were crudely made and looped around its proud neck, and beneath the links flesh that was gouged and torn could be seen as testament to the death throes and the undoing of this magnificent beast.

It stood quietly as though in anticipation of *something*, and then Beth felt movement beside her as Eleri pulled away and drew her face out from the folds of her cloak and took her first look at the ghost-horse.

The white stallion lowered its gaze to take in the scrutiny of this small child and there came over it an almost tangible air of calm. It dropped its head further with an audible snort and the light of fury seemed to leave its eyes as Eleri went to step forward.

Beth gasped and held her back and then Tegid's hand was on her arm.

She glanced at him and he shook his head.

Reluctantly she released her fingers and the child stepped away.

Swathed in her dark-coloured cloak, Eleri looked like a tiny sprite of the night as the pale stallion towered above her like some huge war horse fresh from a field of battle. Hardly daring to breathe Beth and the old man watched as

Eleri pulled down her hood and gazed fearlessly up at the great head as the large dark eyes regarded her intently.

Time itself seemed to stand still as child and beast stared at each other for some moments and then reaching up Eleri's hand suddenly sought the chains that bound its neck. The ghost horse lowered its head further until the chains that bound is neck rattled forward and then, with a wondrous sense of disbelief, Beth and Tegid looked on as Eleri's small fingers found the links, and then she spoke.

The child spoke!

In a weak voice so childishly sweet her words all but danced in the air like fireflies and Beth wept as Eleri's tones picked up strength and found its cadence as she recited a litany so strange and obscure Beth could not define them.

But the old man did, for they were the words of power that would lift the curse, and down the ages had they come, word for word, ear to ear, a surreptitious gift that was given to Tegid's ancestor all those years by one of the gypsies who took pity.

The mist seemed to lift as the child expelled the final words into night, and then, with a sound no louder than the soft sibilance of a whisper, the chains fell away and powdered into dust as a sharp wind rose and blew the remnants away as the very air seemed to sigh with release.

Eleri stepped back slowly her face lit by something almost ethereal as the great beast stamped its foot and tossed its mane before throwing back its head and whinnied its triumph like a clarion call of pure joy!

As soon as the child was within reaching distance Beth drew her in closely as a whole maelstrom of emotions raced through her and she was shaking uncontrollably for *Eleri bach had spoken! The child had made speech!*

Her tears of happiness continued to dampen her cheeks as she hugged her charge to her as everything suddenly fell into place.

Only a child touched with tragedy could break the curse, Teg had told her, a child made in love and yet tainted in innocence. Such a child had been Eleri, and despite her weak and fragile state, she had had enough trust left in her heart to walk out on to an unknown quest and for no other reason than for the love she bore for both Beth and a kindly old stableman.

Neither of them could have been more humbled or proud and then the beast suddenly stepped forward and stopped in front of Teg.

This beautiful white stallion that had once roamed with gypsies and allowed a small boy to ride on its back then lowered its great head and rested it for a moment or two in the old man's hands. It was a gesture of gratitude and a poignant one, and as the old man openly wept the stallion gave a gentle snort before turning and galloping away into the night.

The moon glided out from behind the clouds as the last sound of ghostly hoof beats receded into the mist. Tegid turned to Beth, his face shining in the moonlight and they smiled at each other when suddenly Eleri gave a small cry before crumpling to the ground.

"Teg!" Beth cried and within seconds the old man had Eleri in his arms.

"It has been too much! It has *all* been too much! Oh Tegid, she is not so strong, what have we done!" The young woman was almost beside herself and seeing her distress Tegid cut in swiftly, "Fetch the lamp and calm yourself, Miss, she has merely fainted. Come, hurry now, let us get her back to the house and into a warm bed,"

His calm manner was had the desired effect and as they strode back the way they had come, Beth carried the lamp aloft, her other hand clasping Eleri's as the old man continued to soothe in a low voice.

"You must not be unduly alarmed, she will recover, I promise you. It was a tremendous feat of faith for anyone to undergo, never mind a small child, and she has demonstrated great courage; now perhaps you can see that by releasing the beast, her act of love released herself!"

Beth's heart swelled at the memory.

"It was incredible! I can still almost not believe it, but I heard her! *We heard her!* And although I have no idea what words she spoke, it was magic in itself just to hear her voice!"

Peering at Teg through the gloom she asked suddenly, "How did she know what to say? Did you teach her?" and the old man nodded.

"That day in the nursery; just a few words and then her mind was open," he glanced briefly down at the small face in repose and then back to the path ahead.

"I merely gentled her with certain sounds, much as I would do with the horses when they are upset, and she heard them deep within her heart and so doing accepted destiny."

"Destiny?" asked Beth.

"And willingly so," replied Teg, "The child has more ancient lore in her soul than you could ever imagine, Miss!" He gave her a knowing look, "Forget not the bloodlines of her father."

"There was a druid stronghold on the Isle of Anglesey, I know, but history says that the Romans killed every last one!"

The old man twitched his lips. "Not *every* One . . . Look, I can see the house! Extinguish the lamp, Miss, the moon is bright enough, and let us have silence now until we are safely inside."

Obediently Beth did as she was told and soon they were at the kitchen gate to the herb and a rush of relief went through her. They had done it! Now all they needed to do was get Eleri back into the house and into Beth's room where she could tend to her properly.

She could feel all of the tension dissipating as she followed Teg up the backstairs, the weeks of secrecy, the furtive conversations, all of the careful planning and now finally it was all over, and as they came and turned on to the first landing it was to find Miss Meacham waiting for them and Beth's heart dropped like a stone.

"What on *earth. . . Good God in heaven!*"

The governess stood before them wrapped in her night attire like some avenging angel a candle held in one hand, her face a mask of outrage as shadows jumped all around her.

That she was genuinely shocked, there was no doubt, but as affronted as she was, she still couldn't resist the glow of triumph in her eyes.

"Tegid, I am surprised at *you!* You have always struck me as a sensible man, but *you,* however, Miss Watson. . ." and the tone became contemptuous, "have been trouble since the day you came, and I knew it! *I knew it!* And so did the mistress!"

"Yes, I can imagine you did!" retorted Beth, "But then anyone with an ounce of spirit would be seen as such with a heart as bitter as yours!"

With emotions running barely beneath the surface the words were out before she knew it and taken off-guard Miss Meacham all but reeled backwards. Suddenly the door to Nanny's room opened and she came out tying her robe, her face sleepy and crumpled with confusion.

"Who goes there, and what is the commotion?"

As her eyes took in the scene she looked to Beth, but before the young woman could say anything the governess had recovered herself.

"Well I think *that* much is obvious, Nanny Gwyn!" She pointed a finger at Beth, "*That* girl is unfit for the role with which she was entrusted! Her insolence is evidence of that, not to mention her lack of care for the Squire's niece! Look at her, she looks half-dead! What on earth have you been doing?"

Tegid murmured something to Nanny Gwyn in and she nodded.

"Take her into my room and stoke up the fire, Tegid. Beth, go with him and attend to the child," the old nurse turned back to the governess and spread her hands appealingly

"Come, let us not be hasty here, Miss Meacham, I am sure there must be a reasonable explanation, please, just allow me to. . ."

"I will allow you *nothing*! You'll not talk your way out of *this one*, Nanny Gwyn! I don't even know if the child's alive and *she!*" the governess stabbed a finger at Beth's retreating back, "*She* is responsible!"

Beth spun round her cheeks flaming.

"How dare you! *How dare you,* of *all* people judge me!" she cried furiously, "you have been nothing but vindictive since I came into this house and if unkindness is the creed you're teaching the children in your care then God help them! And think not to show false concern for the fate of Eleri, for we all know how much you despise her, your hypocrisy is as sickening as it is breathtaking!"

"*Beth!*" cried Nanny her face distressed, "Stop, *please,* you go too far. . ."

"No, Nanny, I've not gone far enough! But what matters it now? She'll not wait to vent her spite, nor shall I be here this time tomorrow; she'll make sure of *that!*"

Miss Meacham bristled as she sought to recover her composure. Her eyes glittered angrily and a red flush appeared on her neck.

"Oh yes, you can depend on it, for I will be reporting this to the mistress *forthwith!* I knew there was something going on, all that whispering in stables and creeping about. I have been watching you, Miss Watson, and more closely than you think. And as for *you*, Nanny, quite frankly I am appalled! As will be the master once he hears of this! In the meantime, I suggest that you do your job and attend to the child and tell Tegid to jump to it and prepare the trap."

She turned to Beth.

"And as for you! Go and pack your bags, you will be leaving immediately!"

Nanny thrust herself forward angrily.

"You cannot do *that!* You cannot order her from the house!"

The pale eyes glided down and rested on Nanny's face with barely-veiled contempt.

"I think you will find that I *can* . . . with the master so often away the mistress has come to rely on me more and more, and although it pains me to say it, there are going to be some changes around here in the way this household is run and the removal of the child is just the start of it. And you, I'm sorry to say, Nanny, have clearly demonstrated that neither you nor your judgement cannot be trusted, so I would look to your own *privileged* position if I were you and accept that there may be no longer any room in this house for a nurse, never mind a nanny! Your days are numbered, but then you've benefitted well from the master's kindnesses all these years, have you not, Mrs Gwyn? And this is how you repay him, by allowing this chit of a girl to break nearly every rule of this house and then turn a blind eye when her behaviour threatens the very good name of it! I have to say *I am surprised at you,* Nanny Gwyn!"

The old woman staggered under the onslaught and before she knew what she was doing Beth turned on Miss Meacham her eyes blazing.

"I had taken you for a low creature," she cried, "but not so low that you would threaten eviction to such a kind old woman, and one who has given her *life* for this family! How dare you speak to Nanny Gwyn like that, *how dare you!"*

The governess curled her thin lips, her face filled with hatred.

"You dare to question me! *You*, who have been running round the countryside with the local doctor like some low-born whore, fluttering your pretty eyes and playing the maiden," she lowered her voice and it vibrated with venom, "small wonder the child shows an attachment to you, for you are obviously as much a whore as her mother was so let me tell you this . . ." but before she could finish the sentence Beth lunged forward and struck the governess hard across the face!

"Say what you like about *me*!" she hissed furiously, "But I'll not have you disrespect Eleri's mother, and yes, her name is Eleri, *not* Emily! And listen to me when I tell you, her mother *was no whore!*" she leaned in and the governess recoiled fear flaring in her eyes one hand held to the reddening cheek.

"It is people like *you* who breed hate and envy and who are never *ever* happy with their lot! But mark my words, Miss Meacham; the power of the house you may have, but the power of love you will never know! And so go! Run, tell your mistress! For I have had my fill of you and this house and God help me if I ever step into it again!"

Afterword

It was a beautiful, crisp winter's morning when they came to take Eleri.

As the carriage pulled up to the front of the house Mrs Davis ushered the occupants in to the library where the two solicitors greeted each other warmly having had much previous association. The Squire sat on the edge of his chair looking nervous but he managed to raise a tentative smile as the two visitors entered and they nodded politely before taking their seats.

The day had finally come.

The tension in the room was palpable as the relevant documents were finally signed off.

The mistress was not present. She'd made it quite clear that she did not want to be a part of proceedings and most certainly did not want to bid farewell to the child!

But then nobody really expected it of her. Her job was done.

Between herself and the governess they had ensured, not only the banishment of her husband's niece, but anyone else who had been associated with her.

"I'm glad she is finally leaving and there are worse places than where she is going," she had told her husband archly, "and then, pray; let us hear no more about it!"

The door opened and Nanny Gwyn came in holding the child by the hand.

All eyes looked to the small figure dressed warmly in a thick red coat with a matching hat, but her eyes were carefully lowered, the dark lashes a delicate shadow on the smooth cheeks.

Nanny, too, was dressed for a journey and her eyes looked sore from weeping, but she wore a brave smile and nodded to the Squire who squirmed apologetically.

There followed a long silence broken only by the tall ticking clock and then one of the visitors leaned forward and said, "Hello Eleri, *bach* . . . we have come to take you home."

The little face lifted immediately as the eyes widened with joy, and then with a heart-wrenching shriek she flew across the room and into the arms of Beth who gripped her to her as though she would never let go.

Nanny Gwyn began to cry.

"Oh look, you've got me all going again!" she sniffed and fumbled blindly for her handkerchief.

Beth's husband hurried across the room to the old nurse and offered her his own.

"But Nanny, but they are tears of happiness, are they not? For I have nothing I can prescribe for happiness, I'm afraid, although I confess I would gives my eye's teeth for it!"

There was tentative laughter and it broke the tension.

With a nervous cough Squire Pritchard stood up and offered Emyr his hand

"I would like to congratulate you on your recent marriage, Doctor Lewis, and wish only happiness for you both . . . It is also my hope that we may leave all disagreements in the past where they belong . . . for the sake of my niece."

"Of course! Say no more about it," smiled Emyr and they clasped hands.

"And so I will be losing my faithful old nurse to you, too," said the Squire and his expression was wistful as he took in the obvious affection between the two women as they fussed over Eleri.

"Ah well, it's probably for the best. Galinas House is a cold damp place and things are not what they used to be . . . for my part I would have liked Nanny to have lived out the rest of her days here, but I know how fond she is of my sister's child, and so all changes must come to pass. But I would like to make a occasional visit, if I may?" he added hesitantly

"You would be most welcome." said Emyr and he meant it.

"Then I suppose that all that remains is to say is goodbye"

It was a lively departure as Tegid with Meg in harness brought the trap around with Eleri's and Nanny's things stacked and strapped down securely in the back. All of the servants came to wave them off, even the stiff-backed Mrs Davis, and Beth gave a special hug to Gwen with the promise she would keep in touch.

As Emyr organised the womenfolk into the carriage and ensured everyone had a rug, he then mounted his bay and announced his intention to ride alongside Teg for a while.

"The ladies will have much to talk of," he said jovially," and besides, word has it that Tegid is a man of much wisdom and with all of these women in the house, I am going to need all of the advice I can get!"

Everyone laughed, even the Master, and then with much waving and shouts of *'Pob lwc!'* Tegid took the lead looking smart in his best cap and jacket as his eyes danced with pleasure.

"Is Teggy is coming with us?" asked Eleri in a clear sweet voice.

Beth smiled at the given name and looked happily at Nanny sat opposite her, "He most certainly is, is he not, Nanny? Although I must confess my astonishment that he agreed. I never thought he would ever leave Galinas House! But then, my husband can be very persuasive when he puts his mind to it!"

"And so seemingly can Tegid! He prevailed upon the master to release Meg from the stables so that you can have your very own pony to ride!" Nanny told Eleri and the child's face lit up with delight.

Soon they were away from the house and up on to the moors. The sun glittered on the frosty ground as the horses champed blowing steam through the cold air and they could hear Emyr's voice behind them as he bantered gaily with the old stableman.

"I'm glad you came to your senses," said Nanny quietly, "You'll not have found a better man nor a better match from here to St. David's, and together, you are just *arbendigegdig!* I am *so* happy for you, *cariad!*"

Beth looked into kindly, well-loved face and thought of all of the trials and challenges they had been through together and tears pricked her eyes for the unbending loyalty the old nanny had shown; both to her and Eleri.

The Squire has no idea of what he has lost! She thought with a sudden twinge of sadness, for his children shall grow up with hate in their hearts whilst mine will know only love. . .

"It has all worked out well, hasn't it Nanny," said Beth, "indeed I have to keep pinching myself that it is all not a dream!" And hugging Eleri to her, she added, "Especially now that I have *you!*" And Eleri squirmed happily the dark eyes were bright and busy as though seeing the world for the first time, and both women took joy in her pleasure.

"But what of you, Nanny?" Beth asked after a few moments, "Any regrets? You have been in that house since you were a girl, and if I am to be honest, when we sent our invitation to come and live with us, I was far from certain that you would accept!"

The old nurse gazed serenely out of the window for some time before she replied.

"I have never cared much for unkindness, nor suffered those who would take pleasure in another's sorrow, and if I am to be truly honest; as fond as I have been of the master and his family, so much has changed since the children have grown up. So let us just say that I knew I would be leaving when at the thought of doing so I felt no *hiraeth*."

She turned back and her gaze took in both Beth and the child and with such love her face all but glowed with it.

"The thought of losing you two, however," her voice vibrant with emotion, "filled me with such sadness that when Teg delivered the message we all but danced around the room; for it has not been easy for him either since you left. The wrath of Miss Meacham spreads far, and besides, he tells me he has some cousins near Borth and that he has *always* wanted to see the sea."

"Ahhh, Miss Meacham," said Beth and her cheeks coloured slightly at the memory of their last meeting. "How fares she?"

Nanny gave a low chuckle, "Oh she fares well enough, and ensures she continues to do so since the master talked her out of pressing charges against you. Although somehow I feel certain no one will hear the last of *that* for some time!"

Leaning forwards the old lady added in a mischievous undertone, "But it was worth it just to see her face and as shocked as I was. . . I was also . . . *appreciative*!" She sat back a twinkle in her eye.

"Oh Nan, I would sooner forget the whole incident, I'm just grateful Emyr's aunt took me in that night for where else would I have gone?"

"And by doing so, delivered you straight into the arms of your true beloved, and a whole new life!" The old nurse allowed herself a small smirk, "Oh how the governess must have berated herself!"

"Ah well, it is all over and done with now, Nanny, so let us look forward to a new beginning. And *you!*" Beth tickled Eleri under the chin, "are going to love living by the sea and having your own room! And if you ask your new papa nicely, I think he may even let you have a kitten!"

As the child wriggled with pleasure Nanny Gwyn closed her eyes and the mood was a happy one as the carriage took them further and further away from Galinas House. As they sped across the moors Beth relaxed for the first time in months knowing that she had all that she loved around her.

There was a small tug on her sleeve and she looked down to see Eleri staring out of the window. Following her gaze she saw the most amazing sight!

For there up on the moors stood watching them was a magnificent stallion of the palest hue and on his back, a small boy.

They stared at each other across the distance for a few moments until the boy raised a hand and then they turned and like the finest mist disappeared into the light.

"Was that them?" whispered Eleri.

"Yes, that was them."

"They are free now, aren't they?" said the child with quiet assurance, "Like me."

Beth drew the child to her and marvelled at her simple acceptance after all she'd been through and looked up to find Nanny's gaze steady upon her.

"Did you see them, Nanny?"

"I did."

Beth smiled and shook her head at the old lady.

"I think you see more than you think and know more than you say, Nanny Gwyn! And so let me ask you this and I promise I will never ask again. . ."

"Very well," said Nanny and a small smile played upon her lips.

"Where have they gone, the ghost horse and the boy? Is there a mystery?"

Nanny closed her eyes and it was some moments before she made her reply.

"Why, *cariad bach,* there will always be mystery, for what would our lives be without it. . ? But you just have to have trust, like the boy and his horse, and that when the time is right, the light will guide you home."

Welsh words :-

Arbendigegdig	– wonderful
Arglwydd	– Lord
Bach	– dear /little
Bechod	– pity
Branwen	– Welsh Princess of Myth
Cacen	– cake
Cariad	– love
Cawl	– Welsh broth
Croeso	– welcome
Croeso nol	– welcome back
Dewch ymlaen	– come on
Diolch yn fawr	– thanks very much
Duw	– *God*
Edrycha	– look (command)
Fy nghariad	– my love
Gwahanol	– different
Gwyn	– white
Hiraeth	– longing
Hwyl	– farewell
Iawn	– alright or very
Iesu Grist	– Jesus Christ
Mabinogion (The)	– Book of medieval Welsh fairy tales.
Na	– No
Nain	– grandmother
Nest	– Welsh Princess of Legend
Nos da	– good night
Panad	– cuppa
Pob lwc	– good luck
Seren	– star
Sgwrs	– chat, conversation
Taid	– grandfather
Teulu	– family
Twp	– stupid
Tylwyth Teg	– fairy folk
Ychydig un	– little one
Ydy wir	– yes, indeed
Y ysbryd siarad	– spirit talk